P.Flores

Lunar Faith

Förlag: BoD – Books on Demand, Stockholm, Sverige

Tryck: BoD – Books on Demand, Norderstedt, Tyskland

ISBN: 978-91-8007-941-9

ONE

ACCIDENTS HAPPEN

"Stop fidgeting, I will hurt you with the tweezers if you don´t keep still." Mary was strict, funny considering she was my little sister, 8 years younger and looked like a leprechaun. No really, she´s 5´2 but has the will of iron thanks to mom.

Me? I´m the one fidgeting, my name is Grace (well it´s Graciela) and I´m almost 37, never been kissed (unless you consider camp when you´re 11 and playing spin the bottle with some friends and guys of course) and I´m scared of dating. I´m the kind of girl (yes, I still consider myself a girl even though I´m in woman age) that has good contact with guys, can flirt but never takes the step.

It´s safer to flirt from a far, you only get disappointed but only for a while.

It passes, you learn from it and then you move on to fantasize about some other guy.

But when your family and closest friends, God (well not really), even your co-workers want you to find someone, it means something is terribly wrong with you.

Normally I don´t care what people think, it goes in one ear and out of the other. Yeah, you must listen to them on and on about how you should´ve been married ages ago, had kids and hopefully grandkids by now. What if you never saw yourself like that? What if you´re scared of having kids because of the whole giving birth idea, but you´re even more scared of having sex for the first time.

Oh, did I mention? I´ve never had sex before, yes, I´m a virgin and really have a complex of showing myself naked even in front of a doctor. I´m the one who lifts her shirt, for the doctor to listen to my lungs but never takes it off.

I happen to work as a nurse, I see men every day but then they don´t see me. My co-workers are mostly women and those I have no interest in whatsoever, but there are guys that really have my blood pressure going every now and then.

There´s this guy I met a few years ago: he´s funny, charming and I think he would be a good candidate to be a husband but there´s a problem: he´s dating someone else. Yup story of my life, the guys I like are always dating someone else. Someone entirely wrong for them but still, they do. It´s like they like dating women who treat them badly or whine, feel ashamed of their dorky ways.

His name is Perry, he´s 42 and lives a few metro stops from me. We work in the same building but not the same department, he´s an accountant for the clinic where I work. His girlfriend is my boss, so yeah, it´s a problem. We met one morning when I couldn´t find my keys to the changing room, he had his girlfriends' keys with him, and he opened the door for me. That morning, I didn´t know that he just said that he could help me out. My boss Natalie is a mean person, I can´t possibly understand how she could get such a great guy like Perry. Maybe he likes to be treated badly, what are they called? Submissive, right I read the books about Grey and his weird turn-ons.

I found out about Perry and Natalie after the yearly Christmas party. He was standing in a corner while she danced (yeah, she drinks, like a sponge) and I was on my way home. She had given me the morning shift when most of my colleagues had the afternoon one, so yeah, she didn´t want me to either have fun or sleep. He stopped me on the way out asking why I was leaving so early, I smiled and said that I didn´t have a dance partner. "Then before you leave, we should dance, at least once." He spoke with a loud voice in the noisy club.

"I didn´t know you could dance like this!" I said and we looked like such dorks, but I loved every second of it. Kellis "Trick Me" made our night, he had some funny moves and didn´t mind twirling me around.

A slow dance appeared, and I wanted to leave but he didn´t let me, he pulled me close, and we danced to Europe´s "Open your heart". Funny how underneath the lights we disappeared from the crowd, and it was just us. He mouthed the lyrics:

"Maybe that time has its own way of healin', maybe it dries the tears in your eyes, but never changes the way that I'm feelin'. Only you can answer my cries".

I stayed in his arms, he let me go and suddenly pressed an innocent kiss on my lips. Shocked and didn´t know what to do besides stroking his face and walk out. I got my jacket from the wardrobe in the entrance and left, it felt like I was walking around with a rock in my chest. My bus was standing right outside with only 5 minutes before it was scheduled to leave, I registered my bus pass and sat down. Perry walked out and looked around, until he saw me sitting on the bus that was leaving the street and him behind.

It was almost 8:30 pm, I had been at the Christmas party exactly 45 minutes from door, talk, dance, kiss, and door again. At home my mom was asleep in the sofa, my sister was warming some water for the tea when I got home. She wasn´t surprised, she had always known I didn´t like parties but said that to find my place at work, I needed to become social.

"Hey, you´re home early. Did you have fun?" she said from the kitchen and when she saw my face, she knew something had happened. "Kind of, but not the outcome I was looking for. Can we talk? I don´t want mom to know." I said and went to my room, Mary came after and closed the door.

"What happened?" she said, sitting down on my bed with the teacup in her hand.

I took a deep breath, still nervous after that innocent kiss from Perry "I danced with this guy at the party and before I left, he kissed me." She looked happy, gave me a hug, and said, "Who is he?" I told her that we had met some time ago, that he helped me with the keys. "I still don't hear the problem though, what difference does it make if he kissed you?" I had tears in my eyes, Mary comforted me "Hey, I know it's odd for you but you're beautiful and funny. I'm sure he'll look you up for a date." I smiled, dried my tears and said "I love your positivity, thanks sis. I must shower, eat something, and go to bed. Got to work early tomorrow."

"What? She didn't give you the afternoon shift?" she said, sometimes I could swear she looks like Little My from Moomin.

It was impossible to forget Perry's kiss: it was soft, almost childlike and I think those are the ones you appreciate more than the more adult ones. I remember this one time in camp; a guy kissed my friend Carla and she told me after that it was horrible. Almost like having a worm in your mouth and that I could live without, how could people even find that attractive? Yuck!

As I got out of the shower, my mom had woken up "Hey honey, it´s only 10 pm, did you only stay 45 minutes? I´m going to make a snack, do you want something to eat?" I smiled, a sandwich would be good and some tea. "Yeah, I´m becoming one of those celebrities that only attend a few minutes and gets paid only I don´t. Thanks mom." She handed me the snacks and we went to the living room; it was always more comfortable being at home than being on a party.

When I was younger, we had those "class parties", I usually sat under a table reading rather than dancing. Music was never a problem, I loved it. Mom used to tell me that she listened to all kinds of music when she was expecting me. We watched tv until it was around 11 and then everyone went to bed, but I couldn´t sleep. Perry was in my mind and in my heart.

"Grace!" a voice said as I was entering the building, it was Perry with his briefcase and the sloppy tie. I smiled and waited, now this could be a very good morning. He gave me a quick hug, wow, now this is going pretty well and said "Can we have lunch? I need to tell you something. Meet me at the restaurant downstairs, the waiter is my friend and he'll close a room for us. At noon, okay? Have a great day!"

We didn't take the elevator together but it didn't matter, we would have a lunch date instead! I was in the clouds when I got to the changing rooms and bumped into my boss. Someone was burning the candle on both ends: she looked haggard, too much partying last night and now having to come in early. "Excuse you!" she shouted at me, and I almost got the door in my face. Before entering the room, she pulled my arm "Wait, maybe you can help me." I looked serious at her, I hated when people I didn't like touched me. She let me go and whispered "I need a favor, go to OBGYN and ask them for a pregnancy test. Tell them it's for you and bring it to my office, hide in your clothes." Hm, now why would I want to do that? She hated me clearly and now she wants a favor... Bitch.

"I can tell them it's for a patient, will absolutely not expose my life to anyone. I'll go before the morning meeting, so you'll know where I am." I said and she nodded, I sighed and entered to change. My phone was on silent, it was only 7:45

and the meeting started at 8 so I needed to rush a little to OBGYN. I walked calmly and took the elevator to the ground floor, the girls there were friendly. An older woman helped me "Are you pregnant?" I smiled, No it´s for my hideous boss. She sluts around during Christmas parties and makes me cover for her. But what I really said was "No, I´m not. It´s for a patient, as a favor. She´s really a nervous wreck and I want to help her out." She smiled even bigger, took me to their storage room and gave me a box "Here, bring it to your storage, just in case. They have long production date, so it won´t show the results wrong and if she needs or anyone else help with anything just refer to us."

I thanked her and took the box with me, took one out and put it in my biggest pant pocket, the box with the remaining went to storage. It was now 7:55 and I went by her office first to deliver the test, she took it and put it in her desk. "Was it a problem?" she said and stared at me, I nodded a no and she said "Good, shall we?" showed me the door and we went to the morning meeting. I sat down with the others from the morning shift, a few temps, and a familiar face: Perry was sitting in the background and gave me a shy smile when he saw me.

Natalie began the meeting "Good morning, everyone, hope the ones that were at the party had fun. Today we´ll be fully booked starting 8:30 so please be efficient, oh and Perry from the economics department is here to deliver the list over Christmas bonus. Please see him after the meeting, no discussion over the bonuses. Thank you and go back to work."

The temps got their lists and went out directly, Natalie stood by Perry and was unusually close. Then it hit me like a ton of bricks: she kissed him on the lips and he couldn´t stop her. The possible baby could be his. My head spun around, and I got out quickly, forgot about the list and hid in the bathroom. How could he? The one I let kiss me is with someone else! Tears overflowed my eyes and I sat on the toilet lid, the pain in my heart squeezed it like I was out of breath.

Quiet door knocks outside the bathroom door "Grace, Grace, I´m sorry, I didn´t want you to find out like this. Please, let me in." Perry spoke quietly but I could hear him since I wasn´t crying very loud. "Are you insane, do you want your girlfriend to see us?" I said and he tried again "Please, just let me in. I need to explain." I let him in and closed the door, he looked ashamed, and I could see tears in his eyes. He grabbed my hands and said "I´m sorry, that´s what I wanted to tell you during lunch. Natalie and I, we´ve been together for 5 years but I don´t love her. She´s the daughter of my father´s best friend and this was arranged years ago, during my father´s financial problems. Her father helped mine and then he wanted him to return the favor, he knew his daughter had problems committing and I became the answer. My father knows that I don´t love her but there isn´t much I can do for now, I´m just waiting for hers to leave the clinic to her and then she can let me go. Please, be patient."

I asked him to let go of my hands, and he did, his pain showed in his face, but I couldn't possibly take this now. "I need to get out now, you stay here and go out the door. I´ll take the escape route."

He looked confused and actually not many people knew that there´s a door underneath the sink that goes to the changing rooms. "Can we still have lunch? Please, I don´t want things to end like this." He said before I opened the door, but I really couldn´t say anything besides "I´m sorry, I can´t." He closed the tiny door behind me, and I crawled my way to the changing room. Luckily no one was there, I pretended to be looking for something and got back to the clinic. Natalie was there and as soon as she saw me, she waived me over to her office: "Yeah?" I said and gave myself a quick check in the mirror, looking normal on the outside at least. "Close the door, have a seat." She said and I thought for a moment that she knew what happened with Perry. I sat down on the edge of the seat and waited for the verdict, she smiled "It was negative, so I´m not pregnant. You left your bonus sheet, Perry dropped it before leaving.

I need another favor, could you shop some lunch for me and something for yourself of course. Here´s my card and my pin code 4419." She handed over the card and my envelope with the bonus in, it was always paid in cash and a notice of why you received that certain amount. "Sure, anything in particular you want for lunch today?" I said and she smiled, tapping her flat stomach. "Bring me a burger, everything on and fries. Oh, and a diet Coke."

I got out of her office, closed the door, and checked my watch. I would need to go to the restaurant 11:30 to bring the food by lunch, I need to avoid Perry at all costs.

When I had some free time, I checked my bonus paper and it said 450 euros extra. Wow, normally I get 250 or like my first year I got 150. I smiled to myself; I had earned this. There was another paper inside, a post it: "I´m so sorry, I never meant to hurt you like this. If we can´t have lunch, have dinner with me. My place at 6 pm, the address is: Calle de Los Arcoiris 450 apartamento 30. My last name is Bollinger (yes like the champagne ^^). I´ll wait. XO Perry."

I sighed, at least the envelope was closed and she didn´t see this.

TWO

DINNER WITH INTENTIONS

The day went on, I was downstairs buying lunch for Natalie but I couldn't manage to eat my own lunch. I ended up eating a small package of fruit and stare out the window.

My brain was trying to debate whether I should or should not go to dinner at Perry's. My first thought was no, I can't but then I get that feeling of what if. He could be lying his ass off but also telling the truth and I would just lose the moment.

"Hey, how much bonus did you get?" I was back on Earth with my thoughts and noticed Freddie was sitting beside me, one of my friends and co-worker. I smiled; I never told the true sum of my bonuses since it could be sensitive information. Besides, I didn't believe in the system they had: to rank people's capabilities in money.

"Uh, 275 and you?" I said without more hesitation, he smiled big and said "375 this year, surely comes in handy tonight when I´m playing poker at the Oak Room. Want to come?"

Freddie was single, like me, but hanged with all types of girls. I used to have a crush on him when he first got here but then I realized that he was a horndog, but a great friend. We knew each other 3 years back now, went to dinners and bowled but as friends. He often told me about his conquests of the weekend and sometimes he overshared. The biggest compliment he ever gave me was "You´re one of the guys, I can tell you anything." So yeah, that´s our friendship. "Freddie, you date a lot of girls." I began and he looked so proud, "Have you ever fallen for one that has been stuck in a bad relationship?" I continued, he looked worried for a while and then smiled big "That´s when they realized they should be with me instead. Why, are you?" I looked nervous at him, maybe I shouldn´t tell him about Perry but he as a guy could understand why he was doing what he was doing. "There´s this guy, we kissed at the Christmas party but now it has come to my attention that he´s dating someone.

He told me that he doesn't love her but it's irrelevant. Now he asked me to dinner in his apartment to talk. What should I do?" I said and he listened carefully, he had his serious face on when he replied "I think you should go and hear him out, you if anyone can see people's intentions. You know what you want and what not so it shouldn't be a problem if it's only booty call. When is the dinner?"

My legs were all tingly, but I answered truthfully "Tonight after work." He gave me a crooked smile, patted my back and said "Go for it, you got nothing to lose. Look him in the eyes and see for yourself. Come on, let's go back to work." We walked back to work, so I kind of stopped thinking about him for a while when Natalie approached me again "Hey, I need a favor. Could you go to Perry's office and leave this? It's a leave of absence for me for next week, I'm taking some time off." I sighed, took the papers, and replied "Sure, everything okay?" She looked at me, not with her usual annoyed look but more like it was something secretive "Yeah, it's really nothing. I don't want him to know that I'm going away with one of the doctors for the week to Miami. So, I'm just saying that I have to attend something with my family and he's not invited."

Great, so she lies too! I regretted feeling concerned if she knew that we kissed, she´s cheating big time. "O-kay, I´ll drop it off at his office." I said and she smiled, turned around and went back to her business. Awesome, now I must go and see him. I went to the elevator, pressed ground floor, and turned left, his office was right there "Perry Bollinger, accountant and coordinator". The door was semi closed, and I knocked softly, a quiet "Come in" came from inside and I was trying to restrain myself from telling him the truth.

"Hey, are you busy?" I said and he shined up at the sight of me, got up from his chair and let me sit down before closing the door and putting on the red button that said "Occupied".

"This is the most beautiful surprise I´ve ever gotten, apart from the kiss last night. Have you thought about my invitation?" he said and sat down, I took a deep breath and left the papers on the table. "This is from your girlfriend, she told me to come by." I said and he checked the papers, he didn´t move a muscle in his face but did sign them and kept a copy. "Thank you, huh leave of absence for a week. I wonder which idiot it´s this week, probably the head of neurology.

I´ve seen them together more than once, the woman has no decency." He said neutrally. Okay so he knows what she´s doing, but still, what are we doing?

"I got to go; she only gave me a short moment to leave the papers. I´ll see you." I said and he stopped me, my hair was in my eyes, and he stroked it away. His warm breath caressed my face, I couldn´t move but then again, I didn´t want to move away from him. "Don´t go yet, it´s so strange to be close to you and feel like home." He said, his eyes hid pain, despair but also kindness. I didn´t know how to respond to that so I just threw myself into his arms to hug him and he catch me "Hey, this is a nice surprise. Have dinner with me tonight, if you don´t want to listen, then I won´t chase you anymore. I don´t do this with…" Now it was my turn to kiss him, my childish ways were just to press my lips against his. He looked happy in a surprised way and now he kissed me back, placing his hand behind my head softly and his lips parted mine. For a moment I thought -Oh no, it´s the worm but then, it felt so sweet: his tongue searched carefully for mine, and it was like in the movies.

He finished it with a soft kiss on my lips and I was already out of breath, we smiled and finally he said "I´ve never felt someone so soft and gentle when kissing, it´s beautiful. You, are beautiful."

I stayed in his arms, it felt so warm but then I came back to reality "I have to go, I´ve been away far too long and she´s going to wonder where I am." He looked sad, so was I, to leave him just like that after what we just went through. I pressed one more kiss on his lips and left, not looking behind closing the door. I checked my phone, it had only been 6 minutes, but it was the most beautiful minutes of my life. Now I must compose myself until finishing my shift, that dinner, now I just have to go.

My shift ended at 4 pm, the party people from last night began at 1 pm and my friend Anna was walking in as I was leaving. We talked a little about the party but I didn´t say anything about my kiss with Perry the night before or now. I changed my clothes, checked the phone but only one message from my family "Buy bread on the way home, no hurry. Love yah!"

When I got to the entrance floor, I saw Natalie with the doctor: an old guy, probably married but needs attention from a younger woman. I walked out and checked for the bus to Perry's, texted my sister that I was going to meet a friend and that I would be home soon with the bread. She sent back an XO and I looked at Maps to see where he lived, 10 bus stops or the metro, which would be quicker with 3 stops. I walked to the metro and got off at Barrio Gothic, his building was around the corner from it which is ironic. There's a church there...a catholic one.

I pressed the button for his apartment, and he answered "Yeah?" I moved closer to the speaker and said "Uh, Perry? It's Grace." All I heard was something that sounded like someone was making balls out of paper and then a beep. I opened the door, took the elevator, and got out. He was standing outside, in a t-shirt and pants with a big smile on his face "Hey, sorry, I was making dinner for us. Besides, I didn't want to pour my heart out over the intercom." We hugged, he didn't care about his neighbors seeing us and I personally didn't even know them.

"Come in, make yourself at home. Don't worry, she doesn't live here, Thank God.

Would you like some tea or juice maybe? I don´t drink alcohol, do you?" he said and showed me to the sofa, his apartment was little but comfortable. I sat down, he had some pictures of his family, friends but none of Natalie. In the middle of his bookcase there was one: his father and clearly her father, she was standing by one side looking like Charlie´s Angels.

"What do you think? You like it?" he said, serving me some juice and I looked around. "It´s beautiful, very neat." I said and he smiled, he told me that he had problems with people that weren´t neat in their homes. I smiled, it felt like he was referring to me. I´m extremely neat, my room at home looks like a fridge: everything in order, books and movies, music close to the stereo and my bed is always made. He would probably like it, I thought to myself, and he stroked the hair that had found its way back to my face.

"Sorry, I´m just really happy to have you here that I don´t know what to say. Can I sit next to you?" he said, and I moved a little so he could sit.

He put his arm around my shoulders, and I moved closer to his chest, his heartbeat was a bit uneven, but he could just be nervous.

"Grace, I, I'm sorry I didn't tell you about Natalie. She's not someone you really want to talk about, a mistake I made in fear that her father would take it out on mine. He's old and I don't want to lose him, I already lost my mother 5 years ago." He continued "My father was really good at businesses, and he made a bad call, lost everything, even his house. Natalie's father Luis, took advantage of that and pressed him to engage us. He knows that Natalie can't commit, I know she's sleeps around the clinic but since, according to my father, we're not married she doesn't have to stay faithful. Honestly, I don't care about what she does but I told her before that we needed to end this, she can't until her old man writes the testament to take over the clinic and she can keep it. I'm not interested in working for her."

We looked at each other for a while, he moved his hand to touch my face and I let him. He caressed my cheeks carefully, almost like having a feather pass through. I looked at his mouth, he had a little beard (mostly just markings) and I moved closer to him, his lips moved closer to mine. I kissed him, a little abrupt but he smiled towards me and continued. It was getting warmer; he took off my cardigan and stroked my arms as he intensified the kiss.

He lifted me up in his lap and kissed my neck, first I laughed because it tickled but then I felt that my heart was going to explode in my chest. I sat across him now, he seemed to like it as his smile was even more a satisfactory one rather than the shy look we had at work.

In between kisses, he took off my t-shirt and there I was in my bra and pants. I didn´t feel ashamed, it didn´t feel awkward, it was just right. I did the same and he let me, lifted me up in his now shirtless arms and took me to his bedroom. We landed on top of the made bed, he laughed a little since I almost fell over and said "Sorry, I have no coordination whatsoever. Are you okay?" I couldn´t stop laughing and replied "Yes, this was actually unexpected but funny." He kissed me again, his lips were hot against my bare shoulders as he removed the straps from my bra, placing his head on my shoulder while unhooking the clasp. He took it off, I was feeling a bit ashamed now, but he placed a finger under my chin to lift it up, looking directly into his eyes. Now I could see that they had a hint of blue in them, we kissed again, and our breaths were becoming more and more agitated.

I got up from his lap and he unbuttoned my jeans, I just remembered that I had this floral underwear that kind of reminded of grandmother undies. He smiled, a cheeky smile that I never thought an accountant had. Perry pulled me on top of him, I needed to tell him that this was my first time otherwise he was in for a scary surprise if I messed up his sheets. "Perry, wait, I need to tell you something before we continue." I began and he stopped, holding on to me by the waist. "What is it? Did I do something?" I sighed "No you´re being perfect, it´s just that I have never been with anyone. I´m not sure if I´ll mess up your sheets or something."

He sat down on the bed, I sat down next to him, and he gave me his robe to put on. For a moment I felt like I was going to cry, because what if this is a turn off for him. He continued in silence, moved to his closet, and took out an extra sheet, left it folded in half and put it on the bed. "Don´t worry, I´ve never been with anyone either. I got you covered." He said the words I had been waiting for, but how considering that he and Natalie had been together for so long. "Listen, remember when I told you that Natalie and I were arranged?

Well, I told her that I have my rules too: no sex before marriage. Then I could feel free to hopefully one day meet the one to share my bed with, she knows I live here but she has never been here. The only one is you, yes, I have this silly picture of her with our fathers, but I have it in case my dad comes over. He idolizes her, I don´t. Honestly, I´m going to throw that picture away because it disgusts me when I see her." I was getting chills by his words, he moved closer to me and put his arms around me. He opened the robe, exposing my pale breasts and he touched them carefully, still there was no groping more like stroking.

The same chills went through my body and left me tingling, he got up to remove my granny underwear. I was gaining confidence as I moved up to take off his pants and then his boxers. It was more than clear that he desired me, his erection didn´t fit in his boxers. He moved to my side to pull me down onto his bed, once again he was caressing my body and I felt this weird feeling in my stomach, like dozens of butterflies were waiting to get out.

"If I hurt you, you must tell me, okay?

Promise me." he whispered softly as he entered me, at first it felt like I was having an infection (it hurt) but then it became better, he softly moved back and forth. I breathed faster, so did he and in between we kissed.

We both came and I realized that he was wearing protection, because he didn´t want me to have the pressure of becoming pregnant. He rested next to me, I was catching my breath and he moved his nose to my shoulder, like a puppy. "How are you feeling?" he finally said and pressed his nose towards mine, smiling with his whole face. I turned towards him, facing him now and whispered "Beautiful, it didn´t hurt as I first imagined. And for you?" He kissed me, caressed my face, and sucked in our breaths "Baby, it was perfect."

THREE

DINNER AT LAST

I was getting dressed while he did the same, we looked at each other and blushed. He came over to me, grabbing my waist to pull me close. We both sighed, was this even real? Then it hit me, we were cheating on his girlfriend "I just thought, you haven´t broken up with Natalie yet, so in other terms we´re cheating." He leaned in to kiss me, then whispered "I don´t care about her, I don´t care if she finds out either, we´re not cheating. It´s an agreement until her dad signs over the clinic, she has her life and I have mine hopefully with you now. Can we just, be here now and have that dinner? We´ll work it out, I promise."

I trusted his word, a man like him couldn´t possibly be lying, or could he? All my life, I grew up believing that men lied as they breathed.

My mom, she knew exactly how men worked because she had been there. When she was pregnant, she found out that my dad had another family. She left him and raised me alone, my grandparents helped as much as they could and for some time, I believed they were my parents. Apparently, my eyes looked sad as I was sitting at his table because he took my hand and squeezed it, thinking that I was still concerned about his pseudo girlfriend. "What is it? You look unhappy, you haven't second thoughts about us, do you?" he said with an equally concerned voice, and I nodded, I told him about my family, and he got up to sit next to me. His hands on mine moved to a tight grip of my shoulders, I think he was trying to comfort me, but it was almost like he was trying to take over my pain.

"I'm sorry you had to go through this alone, now I just want to hold you and comfort that fragile heart, tell it that you're not alone anymore. Let me be that person in your life, love me as I'm loving you." His words, it was like hearing poetry and I surely liked it.

We had dinner between smiles, kisses with taste of sugar and then some ice cream when I saw the clock on his wall: 8:30.

I was supposed to be home hours ago, checked my phone and saw 3 missed calls from my sister and one text: Where are you??? "I have to go; my family is waiting and I didn´t tell them I was going to stay for so long. It was very, very nice to be here with you and I hope we can do it again soon. See you at work?" I said and gave him a quick kiss, he pulled me in for a real one and I couldn´t breathe. He grabbed the keys from the counter and said "I´ll take you home, it will be quicker than rushing through the metro. Come on, my car is in the garage." We stepped out, he locked the door and took the elevator. It was a few floors, but he kept busy kissing me, I let him, it´s not like he´s not cute because he is. He´s tall, has dark hair, a few white strains, kind brown eyes with hint of blue, a sharp nose that looks like a shark´s fin in profile, has like unshaved style and his lips are…they are perfect.

He put his jacket on my shoulders, it was getting cold this evening but all I could think of was him: his broad shoulders, some moles aligned over his clavicle, (some muscles but they don´t interest me), his waist hasn´t a six pack instead he has little love handles but see I love that he doesn´t because too worked out guys remind me of Ken dolls.

I smiled to myself when he clicked the car key and a black Nissan Qashqai light up, he opened the passenger door for me and closed it, then hopped in the driver seat.

He had this smirky look on his mouth and I was too shy to look further at him, so I just stared out the window "Hey, you have something on your nose." He said and I looked at his mirror, he placed his left hand on my cheek to move me towards him. We kissed and he took a deep breath out of me, before saying "You Grace, take my breath away." We both laughed about how cheesy that sounded and he start the car, typed in my address in his GPS and drove away. Barcelona at night is beautiful, I still remember when we first got here from Sevilla. Mom got a job as a waitress and my grandparents who already lived here took care of me, we lived there until I was about 10 and then mom met a man who just like my dad hurt her like hell. Andy was American, he was a regular at the restaurant and he asked her out. They dated, moved in together and had a daughter, the leprechaun I call sister whom I adore more than life itself.

But then he became problematic, he drank a lot with his buddies and one night it got too far: he came home, mom was furious since he was supposed to care for us girls that afternoon and she needed to work. Since I was older, I told mom that I could take care of my sister, but she called in sick instead and decided to give Andy a piece of her mind. Unfortunately, he was already pissed when he came home, and mom told him off already at the door. He hit her, mom wouldn´t take it so he hit her again and that´s when he shoved her to the wall and banged her head towards it. She lost consciousness and he ran; I called the cops and an ambulance. He was arrested a few blocks away and didn´t put up a fight, I think they gave him 2 years for assault, and mom filed a restraining order just in case.

We moved around in Barcelona to our current place, near Sagrada Familia where I also work now. We never saw Andy again, which is good since nothing good besides the leprechaun came out of having him close. Mary is the best thing in the world, and we love her so much.

"You´re quiet, everything okay? Do you want me to drive around for a while?" he said, and I turned towards him, his hand found mine.

He put on some quiet music, there was this melody that I had heard before but couldn´t remember. It sounded so sad, which makes it even more beautiful to listen to. "This one is from a movie series called -Fantastic Beasts the Crimes of Grindelwald and the melody is Leta´s Theme. I liked the movies, but this theme is just beautiful." I smiled, "Sounds like a good movie. Maybe we could watch it someday." He smirked, like he liked the idea of us having normal dates in the future.

We arrived at my house, well apartment but we lived on the ground floor. He parked a few meters away and turned off the engine, he kept his hand on mine when he leaned in to kiss me goodbye. "Want me to pick you up tomorrow for work? I don´t mind, the parking lot is around the corner from the clinic if you´re worried that someone might see us." He said and caressed my face, one last kiss before we said goodnight. I walked slowly to the apartment, one last wave and I put the key in the door when mom suddenly opened up "Where in God´s name have you been? I´ve been worried sick! Your shift ended at 4 pm, you had dinner until what 6?" she yelled. Before I could say anything, a voice behind me said "I´m sorry, I kept your daughter away. My name is Perry, I´m your daughters' boyfriend." Oh…shit.

FOUR

SOME EXPLAINING TO DO

"Uh huh, well Perry. Come in please." She said and let us in, mom passed by me to the living room where my sister was sitting and looked serious at us. "Don´t worry, we´re in this together." Perry whispered as he took off his shoes and went in, I felt ashamed, but went in after him. Mom offered him a seat and I sat in my usual place, he smiled towards the pair of eyes that stared at him and said "It´s nice to finally meet Grace´s family, she has mentioned you a few times and I must say, you are great people."

Mom´s angry face toned down, Mary´s question mark too and I felt like I could finally relax. He continued "She didn´t want to mention me before she knew we were serious and we are, Mrs. Gianna. I only have serious intentions with your daughter, in fact, I´m here to ask for your permission to date her." What?? What´s this?

He could've asked me first, well we already slept together so that's all done. I couldn't stop fidgeting in the sofa, something I did when I was either in pain or nervous. Perry got up from his place and sat next to me, with his hand on mine. My legs shook and he moved his hand to it, kind of calming me down. Mom had this big smile on her face, and I could relax "Aww this is much appreciated Perry, to see you towards my daughter, it's been a long time since I've seen love sincere. You have my permission to date her and please, call me Gia."

We both smiled, his comforting made me feel secure and even more when mom came towards us to hug us both. She offered him something to eat or drink but he respectfully declined and said that he needed to head home. He said his goodbyes to my family, and I accompanied him to the door, he squeezed me in a warm hug and whispered "I'll text you tonight, okay? See you tomorrow." Before he finally pulled my face to an even warmer kiss, lips to lips. As soon as I closed the door, mom shouted "Graciela, you've got some explaining to do." And I knew when she used my full name, something bad was coming.

No reprimands from mom, my sister winked since she knew about him but I didn´t share anything about my first sexual encounter with Perry or my first ever actually. I took my evening shower as always after work, only tonight I saw myself with new eyes: every part of me that I could see in the mirror had been his that same evening. My lips were kind of swollen, we did kiss a lot that day and right then I felt that all I wanted was to continue kissing him. Closing my eyes, I recalled that evening, seeing him naked, touching me in a gentle matter, no groping like you see in series or movies where there is no respect. Could this be love, the kind that could last a lifetime?

We watched tv, drank some tea and I went to bed. He had already texted me a few times, that he was home, thinking about our afternoon together and meeting my family. Very happy about everything and that one question remained to be answered: If I wanted to be his girlfriend in secret. In secret meant no one could know, especially no one at work which I considered quite fine. It also meant that we should have sleepovers from time to time but how did that work? Would mom agree? She´s very Catholic, I´m just Christian and I respected God, but we could still have a normal couple life, right?

He sent me an MMS, my wi-fi was not working so I had to turn on the mobile data and saw that it was a picture of him in his boxers, his hair was wet, and his lips were doing a kiss (you know, pouting lips). I blushed in the same second my sister Mary came in, she knew something else was up "Okay, mom bought the whole have late dinner thing, but I don´t. Did you guys do it?" Mary, the leprechaun knew me very well. I nodded in shame, and she held her hands against her mouth, like covering from screaming. She hit me on the arm and spoke quietly "Was he gentle?" I nodded again and she was happy, there were no secrets between us, and I warned her about telling mom that her eldest wasn´t a virgin anymore. That night I could barely sleep, I kept thinking about him and hoped he did the same.

2 weeks later…

It was the day before Christmas, luckily today my shift was only 4 hours and Perry texted me the night before that he had a surprise for me. I didn´t want to think too much but I did hope he would like the shirt I got him. I was leaving some material in the cupboards when I got a text: Can you meet me in the office in 10 minutes? XOXO.

I passed by Natalie´s office, she was typing on the computer so I could sneak away without no one noticing. When I arrived at his office, there was no receptionist or anyone. I knocked on his door and he said, "Who is it?" I smiled, and replied "It´s me, Grace." "Come in." he responded, and I thought that it was a bit odd. As I opened the door I see him, with his legs on top of the table, bare legs and no shoes, boxers, and no shirt on with a rose in his mouth. I almost had a heart attack, closed the door quickly and locked. "What are wearing? Or particularly not wearing! What if it hadn´t been me at the door?" I said and stood by the door, he smiled big, took the rose from his mouth, and put it on the table. He came closer and said "I sent the receptionist home for the day, there´s no one in the office next to mine on either side because they have a boring course in economics all afternoon. It´s just you and me here, oh and I sent a boring report to your boss that will take her approximately 2 hours to figure out. So, want me to take your clothes off or do you want to try out something exiting, let´s say stripping?"

I stood by the door still, trying to understand what he just said: lately we had been sneaking off every chance we could to be together and it was great.

He surprised me every time with something new: pick me up for work, early breakfast, tickets to the movies, visit the zoo, go to church. But this, I didn´t know what to say. "You, okay? Blood pressure? Want me to, uh, check for vitals?" he said cheekily with this sexy tone in his voice, I nodded and said, "Why don´t you help me out?" He pulled my nurse scrubs shirt closer to him and we kissed, he leaned on the small mini sofa chair, keeping his hands on my waist. I passed my fingers on his newly cut hair, moved to his broad, naked shoulders, and squeezed. He groaned against my cheek, I smiled, and his mouth found mine, he tasted of coffee. I giggled when he tickled my neck, so did he when I squeezed his love handles. I took off my shirt and felt his warm skin towards mine, funny how some people get warmer in the winter, I get cold, so he got chills when he felt me but then with his kisses trying to take my bra off, that warmed me up.

We stood there for a while, just holding each other. It was romantic with a quiet tone of piano in the background, he like that, music, or melodies more. I couldn´t get tired of being in his arms, without doing anything else.

His breath caressed my neck, he kissed it, moved his hands down to my waist and said "Stay with me tonight, it´s Christmas tomorrow. I really would love to wake up beside you and celebrate what will be the happiest one I´ve ever had. Please." I took a deep breath, he sneaked in a kiss, looked deeply in my eyes and it sounded so perfect. Really, I had no late Christmas gifts to buy, everything was done already in November. "Okay, I´ll stay tonight but I´ll have to stop by at home to get some clothes. Would you mind?" I whispered and he smiled even bigger, let me go for a moment and showed me a picture in his phone. A big suitcase with a ribbon on, I didn´t get the idea and looked like a question mark. He rubbed my back, pulled me close and said "It´s your Christmas gift, you´ll have to open it to see but you won´t need clothes tonight. So, care to try on the sofa or want to save this for tonight?"

I chuckled, still didn´t understand what he meant but I trusted him. He sat down on his little sofa, with me on his lap and we kissed. He moaned against my ear and said "I don´t know if I can wait until tonight, can we give this tiny couch a run for its money? I want to make love to you Grace."

I took a breath; I could feel that he wanted me, and I wanted him too, but I was too worried that someone might wonder where I could be. My brain said *Screw them, have a moment with this man* and my heart couldn't agree more. I got up from his lap and saw his confused face turn into a face of excitement as I pulled off my scrub pants. He grabbed my butt and kissed my stomach, carefully touching my scar from early childhood, an appendix surgery. My underwear had gone with my pants, and he was happy to remove his boxers. Perry placed me on top of his groin, fully erect and I could barely hold anymore. His touch was still careful, even though we had sex at least 3 times before this time.

I smiled as he moved me back and forth, his moans against my mouth and instant kisses that melted us together.

"This chair was way too uncomfortable, maybe I need to get a couch for two, for your next visit." He said with a chuckle, and I placed my fingers along his back, the tiny moles that I had seen before extended all the way to his waist but only there. I tickled him, he placed a kiss on my collarbone and got my clothes from the floor.

We got dressed and said for the moment goodbye until my shift ended, I still had 2 more hours left. Luckily my escapade had lasted 30 minutes. As I went back, I bumped into Anna, my friend from the other department. She looked worried "Hey, how are you?" I looked normal, at least so I thought "Just fine, you?" "Have you heard the latest? The accountant has been seen with another woman, even though he´s engaged to Natalie." She said and my heart fell on the floor, did someone from the clinic see us? "Do we know who this other woman is?" I said and felt my knees shake like jelly. "No, no one knows her. Only that she´s dark haired, a bit chubby and has really bad taste in clothing." Anna didn´t have any speaking filter: I am chubby, my clothing was more substance over style and yeah, I am dark haired. But she smiled again and said "But it can´t be you right? The guy is a nerd, must be another nerd that likes him. Maybe his secretary."

Annoyed over her comments, I told her I was late for work, and she asked, "You looked flushed, sure you´re, okay?" I nodded, she was nice but no people skills and did not know how to read the room. I got back and Natalie spotted me "Grace, were have you been?

Perry from downstairs wants to talk to you about excessive hours, looks like you're getting more paid vacations or just more pay. He's on line 2 on my phone, talk, I'm going to get a latte."

I took the phone and said, "This is Grace." I heard his voice on the other line, smiled a little and he said "Did you have any problems? Just say yes or no, I know she might be there." I replied "No, none." "Okay, I just want to say that I'll pick you up after work by the coffee shop, okay?" "Okay, thanks." He gave me the killer line before we hung up "Just so you know, the first part of you I'm kissing tonight are your boobs. Byee"

Silly man, I thought to myself, and Natalie came walking with her latte. "Thank you, it seems like he'll send my extra payment sheet to be run asap so maybe I'll have some extra money before new year's." She didn't seem to care so she just passed by me and closed the door, apparently, she didn't like to lend her phone. 4 pm and I was changing clothes, I sent a text to my sister that I was on my way to Perry's and that I was going to stay there until tomorrow. She was concerned that I didn't bring any clothes, so I said that he had bought me something to wear.

"I´ll be home tomorrow before the movie, say hello to mom." I wrote back and she sent me an XOXO again.

I entered the coffee shop and ordered a cacaolat, which in Catalan means hot chocolate while waiting for Perry to bring his car. His shift was only until 3 pm so he went home, changed, and brought the car over. He came in and saw me by the window, ordered a coffee and came to sit with me, looking like a totally different person: no glasses, a white shirt, black pants, and a jacket. The same he wore on our first night. "Hey honey, been waiting long?" he leaned over the table to kiss me, I was surprised but answered his kiss. "You look very good like this, going out?" I said and he clicked his tongue "As a matter of fact, yes, I´m picking up this total babe just now and she tastes like chocolate." I nodded a little, blushed and he smiled "Now that´s the perfect color for you. Come on, I was thinking we could go for a ride before we pick up some food and head home."

He took my hand and we walked out, I opened the door to his car and got into the passenger seat. As he drove off, he turned on the stereo and there was another piano theme "Words".

I looked out the window, during any stop sign he leaned in to kiss me and it was like being in this perfect movie together.

FIVE

CELEBRATING CHRISTMAS

It was Christmas morning, December 24th and it was only 6 am, typical of me waking up too early when I have the day off. I sat up in his bed, he was sleeping and I didn´t have the heart to wake him up. Went to the bathroom and looked at myself in the mirror, I had a bottom swollen lip and a hickey on my neck. Great, explain that to my mom. I brushed my teeth and splashed my face, on my way back to bed I saw his Christmas tree against the wall. Ever since I was little, I loved Christmas trees. I dreamt about being so little that I could fit in the branches and walk around the lights. As I got closer, I noticed a few presents, I didn´t care about what was in more than how the colors looked against the tree.

I sat down on his sofa with the blanket that laid there and curled up looking at the lights. Music, where did it come from?

I woke up and heard Christmas songs in the apartment, Perry was cooking something, but I was still very tired and couldn´t understand what it was. "Good morning, I was worried that you had left but I found you here. Why didn´t you come back to bed?" he said and brought me a cup of tea, bread and butter, different types of cheese. He kissed me and sat down on the floor with his cup on the table, I did the same and we looked like when Japanese has their tea ceremony.

"What are you cooking?" I said and had a sip of my tea, he explained that it was a ham and it needed to be boiled to cook and then he could roast it in the oven. "Normally my dad bought lamb but I´m not a fan, do you, like lamb?" "No, I don´t. My mom roasts ham in the oven, always for Christmas. Is your dad coming over?" I said and he checked the clock "No, not for another 4-5 hours. I would love for you to meet him, but it would be problematic considering. I´m sorry, I´m dragging you to my family drama. Let´s just be together and I´ll deal with him later, eat up, so I can give you your Christmas gift." I smiled, it´s sad that his dad doesn´t let him choose whom he should love. When I finished, he took my hand, we sat on the floor by the Christmas tree, and he handed over a medium package with small Santa´s on the paper.

"Thank you, I brought you something too. Here, I hope it´s not too corny. Merry Christmas honey."

He was blushing, shy and nervous. I opened the package, and it was a mug that said *Girlfriend,* a pair of keys and a picture. The picture was of his closet, with half of it empty. I was confused, what did the closet mean? "It means that my house, is now yours. The closet is where you can save some of your clothes in, the keys are to our door and the mug, well you can use it at work." He said, I couldn´t hold my tears anymore "You dork, I love it! I love you." I threw myself into his arms and he held on to me tight. He opened his present; it was a shirt with matching cufflinks with a heart and a leaf. Now it was his turn to ask questions "What do the heart and leaf mean?" I looked shyly at him, tried not to cry when I said "It means free heart, that you choose who you love. When love is given freely, it will always be true." Perry looked away with tears in his eyes, he turned back to hug me and kissed me so intensively that I could barely breathe. "I don´t care if the Earth breaks down in million pieces, I´ll never regret a moment we´ve lived together. I love you so much."

I didn´t know whether I should cry with him or try to remain calm, I chose to be calm.

He sniffed on my shoulder, and I stroked his back with my fingers, he mumbled something "Sweetie, I can barely hear you. What did you say?"

"Run away with me, let´s forget about the business between my dad and hers, I can start over and so can you. What do you say?" It sounded perfect, just us, running away like in the old days, to be happy. But bills and finding new jobs weren´t easy, not for either of us. I took his hand in mine, he squeezed it in hope that I was rooting for us to run but I needed to tell him "I can´t, we can´t. We´re 2 people in their 40´s, it´s not easy to find something good and lasting. And then it´s your father, what would happen to him? We can´t be selfish in this, trust me I would love to run away with you but we both know that if something happens, we´ll regret it. Let´s be patient, be together here and work out the problems instead. Then we don´t have to hide from anyone."

His eyes understood, it wasn´t difficult to read him up close. "You´re right, of course you are. My intelligent woman, incapable of thinking only about herself, we´ll fight here and be free to live the way we want to. I love you."

I smirked; I could feel his love. It wasn´t just words, it was the way he could compose a phrase. His entire vocabulary was poetry. We got up from the floor, I told him that I would shower and get dressed to leave before his father came. He accepted but first packed my things in the suitcase he got me, I left the clothes he got me in his special part of the closet. He stood behind, put his arms around me and placed his chin on my shoulder. I closed my eyes, it felt so reassuring to have him in my life.

"I wish you didn´t have to go, but at least, I´m going to take you home. Come on." He said and I took a deep breath, before kissing him goodbye here in the place we both belonged.

My family were very happy with the Christmas gifts, mom said "You always know what we need, thank you honey." My phone blinked, there were messages from friends and 3 from Perry. I read in silence "Hey sweetie, hope you´re having a wonderful Christmas eve. I keep thinking about last night, this morning and how much I would love to be there with you. My dad´s here, asking about why I look so sad.

I want to tell him; he deserves to know you´re my reason for happiness. Much love, your Perry." I smiled, on to the next one "I found one of your earrings in the bathroom, put it in your drawer but I think I might need to buy something new to you." Ha-ha, that´s where it was. I looked like a pirate until I saw I was missing one. Final text "I love you, when can we see each other again. Sex is always an option, ha-ha I made you laugh. Love you so much, P."

Mom had served me some chocolate punch and I almost choked on it when I read the final text. I went to my room and took a picture with the mug he gave me, puckered lips, and a small text "Of course, when?" A quick reply with a picture, in his boxers in the bathroom and my cardigan (he looked funny) "How about the 26th, my dad leaves tomorrow around midday, and I can pick you up again. Let me know if you fancy this clothing or nothing at all *wink*. Muaack."

I had this special file in my phone with his pictures, nothing naked just little less clothes on his end. We talked about that when I was in his office, I said that I liked him sending me pictures in his boxers but nothing completely nude.

He agreed that it might get tacky in the end plus nothing to look forward to when we saw each other again.

During the evening we watched the typical Christmas movies: Home Alone 1 and 2, Serendipity but the last one I had no idea which it was because we all fell asleep. I think I went to bed at 2 am, mom and sister stayed on the couch with their blankets. Perry texted "Still awake? Want to talk?" I got into my walk-in closet mess, shut the door and called him "Hey, yeah I just woke up. It was uncomfortable on the couch with 2 more people, so I was getting myself to my room, what are you doing up?" He chuckled quietly "I´m in the bathroom, my dad is sleeping in my bedroom so he can´t hear me talk here. I miss you; I took one of the pillows we had last night to the couch just to smell you close to me. Do you know that you smell like home to me?" I smiled; I think he heard that in the tone of my voice. "It´s Christmas day, merry Christmas, again. I´m so happy to have you in my life, I love you and I must go to bed but we can text tomorrow or in a few hours. Goodnight honey." "Goodnight baby, sweet dreams and we´ll talk around 9. I love you." He said and we hung up, I opened the door and went to bed.

SIX

ALL HELL BROKE LOOSE

Sometimes I hated my job, especially when my boss made plans without asking if I was available first. It was New Year's Day, and I was on my way to work, the clinic is closed but my boss needed a favor. So now I´m on my way to another clinic about 45 minutes away to work her shift until 4 pm (it´s 6:30 in the morning now) and I´m almost there.

My family was asleep when I left and I didn´t text Perry, so he could have some sleep until at least 10 or 11. I was yawning when I saw someone getting on the bus, that I knew "Perry, what?" He sat next to me, put his arm around me and said "I read her FB, she´s on her way home to her apartment and normally she works here at Hospital Clínic de Barcelona every other weekend. How are you honey?" I cuddled up next to him, closed my eyes and said "I´m just really tired, how come you´re so fully awake?

We talked until late last night." He kissed my head "I never went to bed, so I´ll go home after I leave you at work and take a nap, then I´ll come back to pick you up with the car."

When I didn´t respond, he just held me until we were at the hospital then he woke me up "Hey baby, wake up. We´re here." I was a little less tired, but I didn´t want to let him go. We stood in the cold for a while, he gave me a long warm hug and then a deep kiss. As I gathered my breath, he said "I´ll see you later, be good. Oh and, I´ll send you something to keep you awake. Bye love."

I went in, now I was fully awake and ready to work. As I entered the department and asked for Annie, I realized that this wasn´t a regular hospital more like a clinic for aesthetic reconstruction.

"Grace? Hi welcome, my name is Annie and your boss Natalie told me you were coming. Thank you for taking her place, she suggested you for this project work for 1 year. It will take place in Nice; France and all expenses are paid. Your salary will be of 3500 euros a month, an apartment within the hospital is arranged and the flight can be booked with Air France before January 10th since you would fly out on the 14th.

Here´s your validation cheque for that, sign here please." Wow, it´s a big opportunity to travel abroad to work. Right now, as a nurse I´m making almost 2000 euros a month for the same amount of time: weekdays 9 am to 5 pm. But, what about my family? And Perry?

"Annie, this is all very interesting, but I have to discuss a little with my family. Would that be possible? Is there a cafeteria here?" I asked and she told me that downstairs to the right, so I went and called my mom "Hey mom, yeah it was about the job. No, they´re offering me a job in France. Yes, in Nice of all places. Yeah, yeah everything but what about you? And Mary? I´m going to call him, but you guys say yes, right? Okay, yeah. We´ll talk when I get home. Thanks mom, love you guys. Bye."

Mom wants me to go, Mary says the same, but I must talk to Perry. I called him up and he was happy to hear me "Hey babe, how´s it going? Yeah, what now? Sure, sure, I´ll be there in 10, love you, bye." I waited in the cafeteria and soon he was there: happy, anxious and I don´t really know how to tell him that I was leaving.

"Why the long face, did you miss me?" he said with a little smug smile before he kissed me, we sat down, and I brought him a cup of tea. "I have to tell you something, but I don´t know how you´ll take it. The job today, wasn´t a job. More like an interview and a secure job offering in Nice, France. I´ll be gone for a year."

His face was serious now, he looked out the window and then he took my hand. He smiled "Take it, you´ve deserved to have a great job and great pay." He patted my hand, the way he did it sounded like he was both happy and disappointed at the same time.

"What about us?" I said as I felt the tears coming up in my eyes at the same time as my throat felt a lump, normally I could read him but now he was in full lock down. Suddenly he took out his phone and said "What about us? We continue the way we are, except that I´m coming with you. While you were here, I sent an email to my boss and handed in my resignation effective immediately. I have this great idea for a business, and I happen to have a friend in Cannes that can help me out, I´m going to open my own firm with accountant consulting. So, you and I, we´re not going to separate just because you must move. I told you,

I'm not going to let you go." I took a deep breath of relieve, did that mean that we were moving in together in the apartment in Nice? Suddenly there was no time to think any more, he was pulling me up from the chair to hug me.

"So, say yes to the job. Did you talk to your family?" he said as we walked back, his arm around my waist when suddenly he stopped. Right in front of me was Natalie, my boss, and his pseudo girlfriend. "I never thought you would have the balls to do something like this Perry, you still think I can't ruin your family?" she said, it would seem like she didn't recognize me but that was too much to ask for. "And you, you little rat. I'm going to make sure that you never get the job in Nice." She was angry, but not because she loved Perry, it was more her ego being hurt. I felt awful but somehow knew that I shouldn't apologize for loving him, something she didn't do. "I'm sorry Natalie, but you don't love him. I do and if you force my hand I'll have to do something that you'll regret." I said (did I just say that??) and looked furious at her. Her look reminded me of my old boss, the same hateful eyes.

"Are you threatening me, little rat?

Do you even know who I am?" she said, still the same poisonous voice, looking at me like I wasn´t worthy of him. "That pregnancy test you took, it was negative, or did you have to do an abortion? Did your lover ask you to terminate the pregnancy? The same who´s the head of the clinic, whose wife trusted you?"

Perry looked confused, apparently, he didn´t know any of this. Natalie looked pale, she wasn´t so arrogant anymore. She didn´t know that I too had claws to scratch with. "I trusted you with that and now you´re screwing my boyfriend behind my back?!" she said, pointing fingers at me. "You don´t even love me Natalie, do you even know what love is?" Perry said and moved me back, like he was covering me. Natalie took a step back, she calmed down and said "Perry, you know what will happen with your father if you continue this. Do you want him to die penniless? Think it over, you too rat, the job is yours if you let him go."

Perry looked at me, I knew what I was going to answer. "I don´t care about the fancy job in France, you can keep it."

His hand found mine and I thought that he was going to say the same but to my surprise he let me go and said "But I can't let go, my father is depending on me, and I can't leave him like this. I'm sorry Grace, but it's over."

It was like my body froze, everything hurt and my heart burst "What?" I whispered and he told me with his eyes that there was no other way out. I nodded, he chose and so did I "Natalie, I'm not taking the job and I quit. Consider this my weeks' notice. Here's my work ID, you can send my paycheck in the mail. Thanks."

SEVEN

PERRY´S VIEW

(THE STORY SEPARATES)

I was furious over Natalie´s ace in her sleeve, she had always known how to play her cards well. She was smirking with her arrogant smile at me and said "Well, it´s not a big loss. We can find other nurses and you´ll get a raise to stay in the company. My sugar daddy will be more than happy to keep his most loyal worker." I hated her; I hated the situation my dad was in but there was nothing I could do. "I hope you´re happy ruining people´s lives." I said and left; my car was parked in the garage. Somehow, I hoped that Grace would be here waiting for me but no, no missed calls or texts from her either. I hoped that she would reconsider talking to me, I´ll try calling her but knowing her it might be pointless.

As I sat down in the car and started the engine, my phone connected and I said, "Call Grace", dialing up, straight to voicemail "Hi, it´s Grace. I´m not here right now, leave a message and I´ll call you right back, bye." I sighed and said "Hey honey, it´s me. I´m sorry for this, please call me or tell me where you are and I´ll pick you up. Please baby, call me." I hung up and hit my fists on the steering wheel, what could I do so she´ll forgive me? I wouldn´t even forgive myself for this, oh God, what will I do?

I took off, drove the highway to almost reach Barceloneta, parked and took a walk to the beach now frozen for the cold winter. I breathed the fresh cold air, tried to rinse my lungs from the venom I had to absorb from Natalie. Once again, I called Grace but still voicemail, she won´t pick up today, maybe I should stop by her house. Hopefully her family won´t chase me down the street with torches, although I deserve this. I let my dad get me into this mess and now I don´t know what to do about it. Went back to the car and drove to Grace´s home, parked right outside and knocked on their door. Her sister answered, "Hi Perry, she´s not home." But the answer pointed that she was home and that she didn´t want to talk to me, I insisted "Please Mary, let me talk to her. I need to explain, I love her, but my father cannot be left just like that. Please."

Now their mother came over, she smiled towards me and said "Come in, she's in her room but be patient. She's not doing so good." I nodded and walked in, took off my shoes and quietly knocked on her door, opened and she was sitting by the window looking out. "Grace, we need to talk." I said and went closer, she didn't turn around so I took a chair and sat down. Took a deep breath and said "I told you about my father's business with Natalie's father, we're dependent on what she does from here on after. My dad's debt is far larger than I can afford, I've spoken to the bank and they won't give me a loan since my father have loaned against his house. He stops paying and he's out on the street, I told him to live with me but he's too proud and would never accept. He still thinks I'll marry Natalie but I won't, not knowing you that you exist and that you love me. Because I love you and would never let any harm come to you, it kills me to see you like this."

She didn't say anything, I could only hear her quiet breaths and sobs. I got up closer to her, put my arms around her and she suddenly spoke "Please, just go. You don't have any obligations towards me and I don't hold any grudges against you. Be happy and take care of your father."

Grace suddenly faced me and the pain in her eyes broke my heart, her tears were there but she was calm. I nodded, there wasn´t anything else I could say to change her mind. I pushed my luck "Grace, I need one more thing before I go. I know I´m pushing it but I need to ask you for one last kiss, I can promise you I won´t kiss anyone else until the day you come back." Her eyes basically told me I could go to hell, but she came towards me, and I leaned in to kiss her. At first it was one of the innocents, just pressed my lips against hers and I felt her salty tears. Then I couldn´t keep it together and I grabbed her in my arms, but she didn´t put up any resistance. I kissed her again, not very innocent, placing my hands on her face to hold her and she wrapped her arms around me. I smiled to the idea, maybe she was willing to keep seeing me even though in secret but then she let me go and said, "Goodbye Perry."

I sighed, stretched my hand towards her arm and she let me. I left her there and thanked her mother for letting me see her, I noticed some boxes in their living room but didn´t think more of it. Walked to my car, got in and took one final look at her window. She was standing there, and I raised my hand to waive but she closed her curtains and I left.

I stopped at Sagrada Familia, decided to pray for a while. I honestly weren´t very catholic but if anyone could help me, that would be God. Church was closed and I saw an old priest working in the garden, I asked him if I could pray, and he said the underground church was open. I said thanks and went down, it was like a crypt underneath the bigger church. He came in after me and said that Sagrada Familia is in between museum and church but this one, the crypt was for prayer. "What´s bothering you son?" he said, and I sat down next to him, we talked about how I met Grace and how today everything had ended. He took a deep breath, went to a cupboard where they normally had the sacramental wine and got me a rosary. "Here, with this pray every day an Ave Maria and come see me in 2 weeks. God needs to hear you and I´ll help you out."

He left me with the rosary in my hand and went back to the garden, I made the sign of the crucifix on my forehead and went out, he waved at me as I got into my car.

A missed call on the dashboard, realized I never took my phone with me: my dad called. "Call dad" I said, and it dialed to him, he sounded happy "Hello son, do you have time to come by today?

I have a surprise for you." I sighed, I had nothing but time now, so I said, "Sure dad, what time?" "Whenever, I'm here and waiting." I smiled and drove away, the rosary I hanged in my car to remember to bring it home. Stopping on the way to buy something for dad, he liked ice cream, so I got him 2 flavors. A car was parked right outside his house, a car I didn't know. "Dad, you here?" I said and suddenly I see Natalie's father in the living room, why was he here? "MR. Bells, how are you sir?" I said and shook his hand, he smiled, the same smile as Natalie and replied "Good, good, you? I heard you were seeing someone else behind my little Natalie's back, shouldn't do that you know." Ahh, she had already been talking, of course, maybe I should too, but before I said anything she walked out from the kitchen with my father "Hi honey, nice of you to join us." My father looked smug, should've known why he was being so eager for me to come over. "Natalie, what are you doing here?" I said and she came to give me a hug, whispered "Keep up the show, this will interest you." I sat down next to her, with our fathers looking at us. Mine finally said "What was the big surprise you had for us kids?" I looked at Natalie and mouthed "What?"

She put her hand on mine, clawing me with her big nails and said "I´m pregnant." I knew right away that the child wasn´t mine but she continued "And we should decide if we should book a wedding venue soon, before it´s starting to show."

My head spun around, I felt sick over her lies and got up. She was startled and my father looked worried at her acknowledgment, I went back and grabbed her arm. She laughed nervously and went with me to the kitchen "Are you out of your mind?!! That is not my child and will never be, tell them the truth or I will." I said and she was tearing up "I can´t, he broke up with me and said I should abort but I don´t want to. Please, bear with me, I just need some time. I swear, after this you can be with Grace again. Help me."

That was something I did not expect, this morning she was all about how she would ruin our lives and now she wants help in exchange for letting me be happy? Her eyes shifted to worry, despair and I couldn´t say no. "Fine, what is the next step?" I said and she was calm, "I´ll talk about a big wedding, my dad will sign over the clinic and then I´ll release you from our engagement.

But we need to announce it, I´ll talk to Grace, tell her the whole deal. It´s the least I can do." Maybe she was right, this was only a farse to hold up until her father released the clinic to her.

I could only see Grace in my future, us together, being married, having kids. If only she would let me tell her that. I still don´t trust Natalie too much.

We went back to the living room and Natalie announced our engagement, our father´s congratulated us and asked where the ring was. I looked nervously at Natalie and said that we were looking now, but as soon as we had one, they would know.

Dinner went by slow, she smiled at me but all I could do was fake it. After coffee and biscuits, Natalie and her father left, she gave me a quick kiss on the cheek and her father shook my hand. As quickly as I closed the door, I wiped my face and washed my hands.

Left my dad´s house around 9 pm and drove by Grace´s house, no lights and it was a little early to be asleep. I checked my phone and no messages from her, so I called. Went directly to voicemail, maybe they really were asleep.

I didn´t leave any message and went home, took a shower, and went to bed.

I checked my phone again, went through some of her texts and pictures. My heart hurt being without her, she who had entered my life dancing and left quietly. I sighed and was about to fall asleep when I heard a knock on my door, it was nearly 10:30 pm, who could it be so late?

I got up and opened the door, she was at my door. Grace.

EIGHT

A GOODBYE KISS

I was standing outside his door, thinking if this was a good thing or a bad one. Luckily no one heard me sneaking out in the middle of the night, but I put a text message on hold for my sister just in case. I knocked on his door, hoping that he would open now that the door was opened downstairs.

"Grace, what?" I didn't let him finish his question, I jumped into his arms, and he grabbed a hold on me as I locked my lips with his. He backed away with me in a tight hold and I kicked the door to close it behind me. I could feel his mouth form a smile, he kissed me feverishly and I pulled up his pajama shirt to his surprise. "Baby, baby it's not that I don't want this but I need to know if you forgave me." He said as I left him with no shirt on, I stayed in his arms without a word, just continued kissing him so he would be quiet. Perry forgot about the reply and began taking my clothes off, he smiled towards me as he saw my bare skin. His lips locked on my chest, feeling his warm breath all over but feeling cold inside at the thought of never feeling like this again. We moved to his bed, he pulled me on top of him with my pants and his still on. With his free hand he moved on up my body, giving me chills on my spine, kissing my shoulder, my neck and stopped at my mouth. "Baby, tell me…what changed your mind? Just tell me." He said again as I tried to take off his pants, but I still said nothing. When he stopped me, I said "Right now, I only think of how much I want you. Can we talk about this after? I´ll answer anything you want, just be mine now."

His eyes were on fire, I could see the lust in his eyes as he moved on top now removing my pants and I wrapped my legs around his waist. He sat down with me across him and held on to my back, his lips found his way back to my neck as we moved in sync. His moaning against my neck, his kisses, his touch, everything was about to end for good. "Are you asleep? Can we talk?" he whispered and stroked my shoulder, I turned around and placed my hand on his chest. His heartbeat was fast, as he always had after we slept together or if he was in the mood for more.

"I´m right here, tell me." I said but I already knew what I needed to do, he moved closer, so his face was facing mine and I felt his sweet breath warm up my face. "Did you forgive me?" he said again, and I moved closer to kiss him, no immediate answer but a smile.

"You´re not going anywhere, right? You´re staying?" he whispered, and I smiled again, I didn´t want to lie to him but unfortunately my decision was taken. He cuddled up with me and we slept the rest of the night but a little before 4:30 I woke him up and said "Don´t say anything, just make love to me." He kissed me, carefully but then he stopped "I need to tell you something: I´m engaged to Natalie. Just to help her out, she´s pregnant and I need to pretend for the child's sake. We´ll work this out, I promise."

Suddenly, the complicated love I had for him ran out of me and I couldn´t have him close to me. I moved away, grabbed my clothes, and got dressed. "What are you doing? We were just…" he began, and I raised a hand "No, you ruined this but maybe it was in a better way than I had in mind. Perry, I think it´s over between us.

Clearly you have priorities that I´m not part of and it´s good, you do what makes you happy and so will I."

I stood in the doorway and he in his boxers trying to stop me, my tears were making my body tingle and all I wanted was to get back to his warm arms, but my mind stopped me. This was it; Natalie was always going to be in the way of our happiness or maybe it was me who was in the way of theirs.

"No, no Grace. You can´t leave, not like this. I don´t love Natalie but I must marry her in pretense so my father doesn´t end up penniless. I thought you understood the sacrifice I´m making here." He said, holding on to me but when I stared at him, he let go. "Maybe I´m too egoistic but ask any woman in my shoes and they´ll say the same: I can´t watch you marry someone else and be the other. I´m not that person and I´ll never be. I´ll never forget what we had but I have to leave now." I said and closed the door behind me.

Outside, it was raining, and I walked all soaked up to the train station where I dialed up a number on my phone and said "Grandma? Hi it´s me, Grace. You think I could stay with you for a while?

No, no, we´re fine, I just need some new air. This weekend? Sure, I´ll be there. Oh, can I stay for longer than a month? Thank you, I´ll see you soon. Love you, bye."

Well, since I´m out of a job and clearly the boyfriend is no longer mine, I might need a fresh start and what better is that with my grandmother in Sevilla.

I got home; mom was worried since I had sneaked out in the middle of the night "Where have you been?" I looked at her with sad eyes and she knew (God, the woman always knows when you´ve been in trouble). She gave me a tissue, I wiped the tears mixed with rain and said "Well, I won´t be sneaking out anymore mom. Perry and I broke up, he´s marrying my former boss and raise her baby as his. I shouldn´t have continued this ever since that stupid Christmas party." Then it came: the tears, the desperation, and the sadness. My guess is that mom was waiting for that since she grabbed a towel and said "Shower, change clothes and have some breakfast. This won´t do you any good." I nodded, went to the bathroom, and got rid of my wet clothes, showering every inch of what Perry had touched all this time.

Drying my hair, mom was finishing up breakfast and Mary came from the bedroom to give me a hug "I'm sorry, I thought he could be the one for you." I smiled weakly, she had also had her share of idiots before but still managed to stay positive and happy.

We had breakfast in the living room, in front of the tv and I broke the news for them: That I was leaving for Sevilla a while, until I could be myself again. Mom smiled, she had already talked to grandma, and she was happy that I would spend time with her. Since I didn't have a job now, maybe I could even find something there.

Eager to move on from pain and despair, I grabbed my bags and took a flight to Sevilla. Grandma was waiting at the airport, happy to see me again and a little concerned when I told her I was unemployed. My childhood bedroom of my earlier years reminded me of a better time. Old pictures of us, with grandpa as well gave me an emotional start. "Don´t cry sweetie, I miss him too, every day since he left this life, but I know we´ll meet again someday." Grandma said and wiped tears from my eyes, like she used to when I was little.

I took a quick shower, unloaded my bags to the closet in the hallway and my underwear to the dresser underneath the small tv. Luckily, I had brought my portable DVD player to watch some movies while staying with grams, although we usually watched these cheesy tv-series each night.

Grams was making lunch and I came to the kitchen to see if she needed help, but she sent me to the garden to see her dog, Rocky. He was happy to have someone to play with since grams was busy with the lunch making. I sat down on this big sofa with the dog next to me, it had been a while since we had animals to play with if you don´t count the neighbor's dog. It was almost like he could feel the sadness and just laid down on my knees to rest, some people think that dogs can´t understand you but they do. More than a human can. We spent the whole afternoon watching tv, I played with the dog and then called home to say hey to the family.

Perry had stopped by my house but none of them told him where I was, he had already called a few times, but I sent his number to direct voicemail.

"I´m just going to take a week off and be looking for a job in the meantime mom, I still have a paycheck to receive from my old job but then I´m going to start working." I said and mom´s concerned voice on the other end replied "Honey, are you staying at grams period?" I sighed and said, "Yes mom."

A few days later, grams took me out to their closest shops and one vegetable and fruit shop. She greeted the vendors who were more than happy to talk to her, weren´t really that interested in why I was there. "Who´s your company Mrs. Fiorella?" one said, young guy in his early 40´s, grams proudly said "My granddaughter Graciela, she´s staying with me for a while." I smiled; my sunglasses kept my cool but underneath I was sweating like a pig. The young guy with the smirky smile said, "Is she a tourist?" thinking maybe that I didn´t understand the language and I felt the urge to respond, "Actually no, I live in Barcelona though, but Sevilla is my hometown." He almost dropped his jaw; do I look like a tourist?

He gave me a cheeky smile and said nothing, so I went looking for the cherries and he stopped by "Miss Graciela, have some cherries on the house." He gave me a bag to fill, I said my thanks and said "Please, just Grace. Grams always calls my full name." He smiled again, whispered "You don´t remember me, do you?" I was confused, did I know him? "I´m sorry, I don´t. From where?" I said and he went back to the counter, whispered something in his colleagues' ear and he laughed a little. Feeling awkward I went to the counter and said: "Should I remember? I moved when I was little, are you someone who I went to school with?" He kept smiling, but he didn´t remind me of anyone from back in the day.

"I have a bad memory but if you told me your name maybe?" I said and, in my head, it sounded like I was pleading to him, why was I even doing that?

"I´ll give you a clue, next time you´re here, I´ll tell you my name and from where. But if you remember first, I´ll buy you dinner." He said and blushed, now so was I. My legs were becoming jelly, it was hot in the store and sweat was running down my cheeks. He finally said, "Chocolate wafer" and laughed, I still didn´t know who he was, and it was a stupid bet, but I was going to ask grams if she might know.

"Chocolate wafer, great, that´s it? Thanks for the cherries." I said, he kept smiling but nothing worked in my head. When we walked out, grams said "Remember when you were little? Outside of school there was a little boy who sold chocolates with his grandfather. It´s him." Oh, but he didn´t go to school with me though. He worked there when the other kids went to school. "Grams, is it Gabriel?" I said and remembered everything:

There was a boy in a very small kiosk with an older man that sold chocolates, chips, and other things to eat before, during or after class. A flash back of my younger days when grams took me to school and bought a chocolate from the little boy outside. I also remembered once talking to him about why he didn't attend school and his grandfather said that his family couldn't afford it.

The feeling of having a privilege to be able to study, to move to a bigger city and become a nurse, not all people could do that. "Don't be sad honey, Gabriel could study years later after you left and now, he was his own business. Not a fancy one but he's happy." Grams said and she stroked my back, I think I still remember how much I cried when he one day left the stand. We got home and I went to wash my hands before washing the cherries, they were sweet and tasted like summer and I noticed a small piece of paper at the bottom. Maybe someone had forgotten a receipt or something, I unfolded the paper:

Hey Tourist!

I´ll bet you don´t remember me, but I do remember you. This is my telephone number +347421122111, in case you remember, and we can talk about that dinner. Kisses the vendor.

My cheeks turned tomato red, and I had to hide for a minute in the bathroom. Gabriel was cute, I think grams still has the picture we took when we were kids. I got out, went to the bookcase, and checked the photo albums from 1987.

"Grams, come and take a look!" I said and showed her the pictures from those days, she changed glasses and said "Ahh yes, there you are with Gabriel just outside of school. You were great friends, and you found it very unjust that he couldn´t attend.

I remember when it was a campaign to help an orphanage, you didn´t want the raised money to go to them but to Gabriel´s family. They were poor but very proud and refused the help, that´s when he left."

It was all coming back to me; I ruined his life with my help. The tears were coming back, and she comforted me "It's not your fault, sometimes people don't want help from others and there's nothing you can do about that. He's fine now and I guess he owes you dinner." She chuckled, put on the kettle and we had some tea. Later, I typed his number on my phone and dialed "Hi, I'm looking for Gabriel. This is the tourist." He laughed, there was a sweet tone in his laughter "Hey tourist, how are you? You found me at last, I believe I owe you dinner." I blushed and it felt like he knew that I was "You don't owe me anything if someone owes something it's me. I ruined your life, meddling in something I didn't even understand." He sighed over the phone, then a happier tone "No, you did everything that no one else was capable of, not even my own family. When they left me with my grandfather, he was all I had. He died, 15 years ago and to this day I miss him. Now I have my own business, and everything is fine, don't worry. Let's talk about that dinner then, how about Friday at 5 pm? There's this great place called "Tortillas" that has the best buffe in town, we could have dessert at the Ben & Jerry's after."

I was trying to hold my tears and when he said dessert, they went away, I couldn't help but smile. "Sounds good, were do we meet?" I said and he chuckled over the phone, it was like having dinner plans with a good friend. "I´ll pick you up at your grandma´s or do you want to meet outside of our old school?" he said, and I chose the latter, we said our goodbyes and grandma was looking all sneaky "So, you have a date on Friday."

DATE & THE MOTORCYCLE

I didn't walk fast, but before 5 pm I was already there walking slowly around the corner.

Grandma had teased me all day for this date, she thought it was cute that he did it this way, even though the memory flashes of me as a child fighting for someone else's rights still were a bit blurry. The store was closed, and a motorcycle was outside, parked right by the sign that said todays offers. It was a beautiful black Kawasaki Ninja; I had only seen it before in pictures but never live. I didn't even hear someone behind me saying "I hope you're not scared of riding it, this is our transit today." "Hi, maybe it won't be such a good idea. How do I know you won't drive like a maniac?" I said, feeling a little adrenaline flowing through me at the mere sight of riding this gorgeous bike. "I can see the glitter in your eyes, here this one is for you. I promise that I won't hurt you, try to relax."

He said and handed over the black helmet, I put it on and sat behind him. I prayed in my head that it wouldn't be too scary, but as soon as he started the bike, I was regretting coming here in the first place.

"You ready? Hold on tight and try not to close your eyes." He said and we rode off, it was a frightening experience but the rush of flowing through the streets. I didn´t close my eyes and I gripped my hands on his waist, enjoying my ride. We stopped at this little place, where he parked and helped me off.

The helmet got stuck and he was laughing so much that I couldn´t stop either. "Here we go, hello doll face. You, okay?" I took a breath, and his hands were cupping my face, for a moment I thought he was going to kiss me, but he only removed a lock of hair stuck to my eyes and took the helmet, placing it on his bike. He locked it and we went inside, opened the door for me and I was surprised to see him so nervous when I looked into his eyes. His brown eyes seemed bothered by me looking at him, so he looked away and greeted the waiter with a brotherly handshake "Hey Juan, how´s it going?"

The waiter, was very happy to see him and suddenly took a notice to me "And this pretty thing?" I smiled and said "Hi, I´m Grace, I´m

Gabriel's…" What am I? His date? His friend? I didn't have time to think anymore until Gabriel blurted out "She's my date. You think you can score us a nice table and the menus?" My cheeks were burning, it wasn't embarrassing but I was still shaky after his quick response, was this a date date or was it get to know each other date?

Waiter Juan showed us to a table by the window, Gabriel pulled out my chair and I sat down, took the menu, and looked. "Juanito, could you get us a pitcher of beer. Nonalcoholic please, driving the babe today." Did he just call me babe? Juan smiled and went back to the kitchen, I put down the menu and said, "Did you call me babe?" He chuckled "I meant the bike, but if you want, you could be my babe too. Just say the words honey."

I realized he was kidding, pouted a "Yeah right" and suddenly he got up from his chair, quickly planted a kiss on my pouting lips. "What are you doing??" He smiled and said "What, I thought you were inviting. Sorry, my bad."

I don't know if my face was furious or if he was just teasing but he couldn't stop smiling and I didn't know what to do.

He sat down again and said "Sorry, I think I just winged it. My apologies, I don´t want you to feel uncomfortable now. Let´s just have a good time, okay? Don´t overthink it."

Great, now I´m just a "good time". I kept looking at the door and thought about just leaving, then the tears came. It wasn´t a good idea to come here with him or to accept his proposal in the first place because my heart was still broken.

Gabriel´s eyes met mine and his cocky smile became a concerned o, he got up from his chair again, put his arms around me and whispered "I´m sorry, I´m not very good at being someone´s date because I don´t date at all. Please, forgive my bluntness and for this." He leaned in and kissed me, it felt like a butterfly was touching my lips. His smell of aftershave tickled my nose, and his hand was reaching for my face. He caressed my chin, my nose, kissed my eyelids and then whispered "You´re not just any girl you know, I´ve dreamed about this for years.

I´ve liked you since the first day of school when you bought a chocolate bar from my grandads stand and shared it with me. I knew that you were special." I could barely breathe; it was a beautiful declaration of love and suddenly there was no one else there apart from us.

"Gabriel, I, I don´t know what to say. I recently broke up with someone and I don´t even know if I´m ready to date someone new. If you could give me time..." I began and he put his head next to mine, like he was trying to hear my mind speak directly to him. "Don´t worry, I´ve waited a long time to just see you again. I can wait more for you to be comfortable around me as well." He gave me a little smile and went back to his seat, just in time for the pitcher of beer to come in. There was also a pitcher of iced tea with lemon wedges inside, and he gave me that cheeky smile. "Cheers to a new beginning." He served me a glass and took one for himself, we clinked the glasses, and he took a deep breath "So, how was your life in Barcelona? What do you do there or did?" I told him that I was a nurse, that I worked in a clinic but then I quit because I had fallen for someone that wasn't right but still managed to have a relationship with.

Gabriel listened, he smiled from time to time and then said "I´m sorry, but that guy used you. He knew that he had to marry someone else but still managed to trick you into a relationship that he knew didn´t have a future. That´s nasty. I´m glad you left him." I blushed, not because he was being nice to me but how stupid my relationship with Perry was. Gabriel was right, he did use me knowing that he couldn´t have it any other way but still could have some fun in the process.

"Yeah, I feel pretty stupid now. I guess when you think someone loves you, you never suspect that they might be fooling you. What about you? Ever met that one true love?" I said and he leaned over the table to whisper "I´m looking at her, she just doesn´t know it."

The food arrived (Thank God) and he offered me some chili nachos, but I declined "No thank you, I´m allergic to chili. Would you like some of my grilled chicken?"

He licked his finger after eating one of the nachos and said, "No thanks, but I´ll tell you something else I would like to taste." He winked and there was tomato face back in the game again.

After the dinner, we walked a little. There was this huge park and we sat in a bench, he put his arm around me and said "Well this wasn´t so bad, right? If you want, you could have it all: I work hard, make quite good money even though my job isn´t that fancy and I have absolutely no commitments with anyone else. But if you chose me, everything is yours. I´ll love you forever and beyond if that´s what it takes. Take your time, I´m right here."

We watched the sun set and went back to the motorcycle, he handed over the helmet and I put it on. I grabbed his waist and he turned on the engine, now I wasn´t at all scared to ride, it was a relief.

Back outside the store and he turned off the engine, I got off, took off the helmet and gave it back to him. He didn´t remove his but opened the shield "Thanks for the lovely company and I´m sorry if I offended you in any way. Want me to walk you home?" I smiled weakly but I didn´t need company. I took his hand and gave it a squeeze before thanking him for the dinner "Thanks for the dinner, it was nice to see you again and know that I wish the best for you. Goodnight."

He pulled down the shield and turned on the engine but didn´t drive away until I walked away. I felt the urge to go back, I wanted to kiss him long and hard to remove Perry´s image from my mind. I checked my cellphone; it was now 9 pm. I never told grandma how long I was going to stay out, so I still had some time, I ran back but he wasn´t there anymore. I went past the store and nothing, but an old lady asked me "Looking for someone dear?"

I smiled and said, "Sorry ma´am, have you seen Gabriel?" She looked surprised and said "Yes, he lives in the apartment across the street. 2nd floor, last name Rodriguez." I thanked her and went to the building across, checked the names and suddenly someone appeared behind me "Hey, looking for me?" Gabriel had been parking his bike in the garage a few meters away and had just come back, he wasn´t wearing his helmet anymore but had it in his hand. I threw myself around his neck and he dropped the helmet on the ground "Woah, hey." Suddenly we were face to face and I couldn´t resist him anymore, so I kissed him. At first it was awkward since I accidentally bit his lip because I was too eager but then everything was just flow. His lips tasted beer (not a fan) but I didn´t care, he pulled me towards the wall, and we kissed for a long time. Suddenly, when we were out of breath he said, "What happened to - I need time?" I knew he was teasing me, so I responded, "Forget about that, can I come up?" He smiled, this crooked smile, and he opened the door.

We ran, literally ran up the stairs and he opened the door to his apartment, let me in first and put his arms around me from behind. Gabriel kissed me on the neck, held his arms on my sides and I turned around to kiss him.

He smiled in between, I said "I need to get back to my grams by 10 pm, could you take me home then?" A cheeky smile appeared, and he said, "What can we do here for 45 minutes?" Now it was my turn, I locked my lips on his as I removed his denim jacket. He cupped my face in his hands and kept kissing me as I now took off his shirt, button by button. I pushed him towards the sofa, and he fell on it, in a sit right position with me on top of his groin. His shirt flew across the room, and I kissed his neck, moaning against his ear since he was working on mine.

Gabriel lifted me up in his arms, carried me to his bed and put me down.

I was about to take off my shirt and he whispered, "Allow me." I moved my hands to the sides, and he lifted them up, he was cold, and my skin turned into chicken skin within seconds. He put my shirt on a chair and admired me sitting on his bed, in a bra with my jeans still on. He smiled as he unbuttoned my jeans and left me there with only underwear, as he took off his, throwing them on the floor. He took my hand and I stood up, then sat down leaving me standing, his hands grabbed my butt, pulling me closer so he could place his mouth on my belly.

"It tickles." I said and he smiled, removing my underwear slowly, taking in every inch of my naked skin that was only a breath away from him. Gabriel sighed, as he pulled me down onto the bed on top of him, stroking my bare thighs, forming my legs along his. The clock on the wall clicked, it had been 15 minutes since we barged in here and still hadn´t done anything else than just look at each other apart from touching of course.

"Stop staring at the wall, I´ll get you there in no time. Now, want to try something different than your average sex?" he said in a low, sexy voice.

I didn´t know what he meant, hopefully not some weird sex thing because honestly, I did well with the regular.

I nodded and he moved on up a little, at eyesight of my breasts. His warm breath kept me on edge, but he never moved closer than that, it was almost like he was only teasing me. "Are you teasing me?" I said and tried to pull him closer, he took moved up his hands to my waist to keep me still. "The point of this is that sweetheart, you're not supposed to feel anything else apart from me teasing your body." Gaaah! His voice made everything worse, it was seductive and provocative.

He stood up now, looked me in the eyes and whispered "Now, I'm just going to kiss you. Nothing more and nothing less because we don't have time for more." I checked the clock again, we had approximately 20 minutes and I winged it by pushing him onto the bed, climbing on top of him. If he didn't want to have sex with me, then we won't but I will show him what I'm capable of. Gabriel laughed quietly and I said, "Oh so you think this is funny, I'll show you funny."

I kissed him, not aggressively but hard enough to make him catch his breath, his arms above his head and he couldn't wait either: he moved them to my waist and wrapped me in a hug. I giggled against his ear, nibbled it and he groaned "You're not being that sweet little girl anymore, I think I underestimated you." I smirked as we now switched places and he kissed my neck, giggling in between since I was stroking his back noticing a tattoo on his left shoulder blade: a wing. "Tell me about your tattoo." I said and kept stroking it, there was a slightly porous are underneath it.

He moved to my side "It´s an angels wing, I guess because I always wondered what happens in the afterlife. Do you have any tattoos?" He stroked my chin, my arm and placed his hand on my side "No, I haven´t any. Always wanted one though but I don't really know what to get. Did you do it a long time ago or?" I moved closer to him, and he turned his back to the bed so I could rest on his chest. He sighed, put his arms around me and said "Well, I guess my grandfather, the one I worked with outside school is the one that inspired me to get one. He had this sailors tattoo on his forearm, and I promised him to get something that meant something to me, so I did. He meant the world to me and when he passed, I lost track of everything. He was my father in so many ways and I really hope that he can see what I´ve done with my life, what a great girl I´ve met again."

My tears reached his chest and he pulled me up a little to kiss me, comforted me in his arms and we didn't do anything else besides being there in that moment.

We got up, got dressed and he handed me his helmet, the same I wore earlier "I guess this one is yours now, want to take it home or do you want me to have it?" I took it without hesitation, wrapped my arms around him and we kissed again. You would think I was frustrated about no sex when we were supposed to, but I think I liked this teasing thing, made me feel like I want him even more. I sat behind him on his motorcycle, wrapped my arms around his waist and he drove off. Since you can barely hear anything, we didn't talk, we waited until we arrived at grandma's house and she was...at the door "You have some explaining to do missy. Get inside, say goodbye to your friend." I sighed; she was right. I needed to respect her home, be there at a reasonable time and even though 10 pm wasn't that late, still, it was her home and her rules. "Goodnight, Gabriel, thank you for dinner and the ride. I'll text you."

I said and gave him back the helmet, but he returned it to me saying "Keep it, it's yours now. Yeah, I'll look forward to it oh and if you get grounded, let me know. I have some ways of communicating." He winked and gave me a quick kiss on the cheek, lucky grandma didn´t see that I was burning up. He waved quickly to grandma, and she waved a "go away", we walked in, and she shut the door behind me.

"I was worried, thought you got lost or something. By the way, your mom called and wondered what you were doing, I didn´t say you had a date but call her. Want some tea?" she said and walked to the kitchen, I washed my hands and said "Sorry grams, we lost track of time. Won´t happen again, uh yeah a big cup please and I´ll call mom now." The phone rang, no answer so I tried again, this time she responded, "Hello honey, how are you?" We talked for a while, I told her that I was out with a new-found friend from the past and she said "Who´s that? Where did you meet?" So, I told her, didn´t say anything about the ride home nor the encounter in his apartment. Finishing our conversation, she said "I hope you come home soon, we miss you."

E L E V E N

U N W A N T E D   V I S I T O R

It's been 6 months since I've stayed with grams, we got along fine, I've started a new job and well dating Gabriel exclusively isn't bad. We've developed a whole new kind of relationship where we don't have any traditional sex but practice more teasing, apart from kissing of course. He picks me up for work every morning since we're now working together, I changed career paths to develop his fruit/vegetable business with delivery and online shopping. Which he absolutely loves and feels much more comfortable especially for the elders that has trouble going out or busy families that have kids and no time to shop.

Grams came to terms that I like him, we like each other, and he adores her, she's very fond of him too even though she wouldn't admit it because "men tend to become spoiled". I call mom three times a week and she's coming to visit soon with my sister.

Besides, I've told her about the dog and she's more than willing to take a flight here during vacation season.

I was working with the computer inside the store, Gabriel was putting some fresh fruits on the stands, and he peaked in from the doorway "Hey, tired? You know, our siesta today, we could do something." The look on his face said it all, another teasing session which is fine by me but someday I would like to have traditional sex with him as well "What do you have in mind?" I said and bit on the pen that I had in my hand, he came in and I notice that his shirt is slightly open. I pulled him towards the wall and buried my head in his neck, he laughed, cupped my face to kiss me when we heard the doorbell "Silly customers" he hissed and gave me a quick kiss again before he went out.

A man spoke to him, I barely heard the voice, but Gabriel came back inside and said, "Uh Grace, there´s a guy out here, says he´s your boyfriend." I froze, I didn´t have a boyfriend but one ex that might have not understood the "we´re done" part... I got out and there was Perry, with sunglasses and a big smile when he saw me. "Hey, your grandmother told me you worked here.

Can we go somewhere to talk? Please." I didn´t like when he plead, it gave me guilty conscience even though I had nothing to feel guilty about.

"Yeah, there´s a small park nearby. Wait outside, I have to talk to my boss." I said and he walked out, while I tried to make Gabriel listen "I´m sorry, I broke up with him a while ago and we haven´t spoken more since. He knows it´s over, I´ll just be clearer, okay? I´ll be right back, don´t be mad." Now suddenly I was pleading, and Gabriel was pissed, I could tell because normally he kissed me back but now, he just pouted. I decided to give him a preview of what we could do later, I took his hand and walked back to the room where the computer was. Luckily, we didn´t have any customers besides Perry that was waiting outside and wasn´t really a customer. The couch where we usually had our siestas became our improvised bed: I pushed him onto it, opened my blouse, to his surprise I wasn´t wearing a bra underneath and frankly I didn´t need to since my breasts were quite firm (no silicone, thank you very much). He didn´t do anything at first but when I opened his shirt, he couldn´t stay mad at me and grabbed my butt firmly. I laughed a little, what! it tickled when he did that, I kissed him feverishly and to feel my skin against him made him aroused.

He breathed hard against my ear, and I bit his neck gently, stopping before it went too far "Hey, save this for later. I wanted you to know that what

I´m about to do with my ex is just talk, this is saved for us, for later." I buttoned my blouse and he groaned but smiled sweetly as ever "I know, I trust you. Go now." I gave him a quick kiss and went out, when Perry asked why I had taken so long I said, "I needed to tell my boss who you were and why you were bothering me at work." Perry seemed different somehow, his sunglasses had been covering his swollen eyes, like he had been crying the night before. "So, want to tell me what you´re doing here?" I sat down at the nearest bench and sat next to me, it didn´t bother me to have him close but this weird warm feeling was taking up my heart. Of course, he was important to me, he had been my first real boyfriend and even though it didn´t work out, I didn´t hate him for it.

"I miss you and I´m truly sorry for what happened with Natalie, but you have to understand that my hands are tied. No jokes please, I´m serious, my father depends on hers and there isn´t much I can do. And there´s something else, we´re getting married in a few months. It´s not for real though, but I don´t know how much help me telling you that if you´re not interested in listening." He said and kept his head down, I sighed, things had not changed in his life, but they had in mine. "I´m sorry that you have to marry someone you don´t love but trust me, no one could ever get that. Would you understand me if I married someone else for other reasons? You work, even if the department fired you, you could find something else. But you´re afraid and I can understand that." I said and he couldn´t keep his tears in.

"What do you want from me? I´m not as strong as you, I can´t take off like you did, find someone else to love and then just live my life. I´m sorry but there´s other factors that you couldn´t possibly understand because you´re too selfish." I kept calm at his interesting choice of words, I knew he didn´t mean it or maybe he did, honestly, I didn´t care and I didn´t come here to be lectured.

"Listen Perry, I wouldn´t have minded if you had gotten her pregnant just before we met. But to use her behavior as an excuse to break things, I won´t accept that and you know maybe you two belong together. You seem to have a knack for lies and deceit." I said and walked away, back to Gabriel at the store.

He was finishing unpacking some groceries and I locked the door behind me, put the sign "Closed" on the door and grabbed his hand. "Hey, we still have another hour to go before the siesta." I lead him to the sofa, pushed him down again and laid on top to kiss him. He held on to my waist and said, "I don´t want to push it but what are we doing?" I looked at him with a bothered look and he just shrugged his shoulders to continue kissing me, I opened his shirt and snuck in my head to taste his warm neck. He groaned against my ear, just like earlier but now it would seem he wanted more than just a simple teasing session…

"Can we move this to a more comfortable place? Let´s go to my apartment, we can spend the whole afternoon there until we open again at 4 pm…come on!!" I opened the door, he closed and locked, ran across the street to his place.

This time, he opened the door, and we kissed our way into his bed. I sat down and he took off his shirt, moved down to the bed to undress me but I rather did that myself: I let him sit there, bare chested, to watch me undress in front of him. His eyes were dark, small sparks of fire that ignited at the sight of my naked body, and I could see that he liked what he saw.

Gabriel grabbed my waist; I fell onto him, and he quickly moved around so I was underneath. His hand caressed my face, I closed my eyes to enjoy his touch as it moved along the curves of my breasts to my belly and back again to my face. He followed the lines of my hips, to the outside of my knees, the inside of my thighs and back up again. His touch felt like getting bitten in the neck by a mosquito: thrills all along my spine. So far it was still a teasing session, I was being turned on but not really addressing my carnal feelings until he suddenly unbuttoned his jeans (to my surprise) and made the move on me. He wasn´t careful anymore, it was raw and hot, like he had been saving himself all this time and now he had just let go, we moved in sync, so our bodies ended up becoming one and when we finished, we stared at the ceiling, catching our breaths. Gabriel smirked, I could see from the corner of my eye, and I turned over to his side to ask what he was smirking about "Tell me something, why didn´t you want to have sex with me the first night when I basically threw myself at you?" He blushed, maybe he wasn´t the ordinary guy that thought about sex all the time but was averagely interested?

A sigh escaped his mouth and he turned over to face me "Because I don´t want to be your escape from your ex, I want to be the one for you, because I´m not the kind of guy that jumps any girl. It bothered me today that he still refers himself as your boyfriend even though you broke up with him, when we were in the pantry about to have sex, it felt like you were on to me to provoke him." I turned back to my side, maybe he wasn´t that off from the truth but I didn´t have the same feelings for Perry anymore. In fact, seeing him today didn´t bring anything back apart from anger that he´s such an idiot, gullible and that he ruined us to please someone else. I sat up, covered myself with the sheets and put my feet down on the floor, Gabriel sat behind me and wrapped his arms around me, kissing my shoulder, whispering "I don´t mean that you´re in love with him still, more like things needed to be said and that´s what you did today. I can feel your heart and I know it beats more for me than for him and I wouldn´t blame you for caring, I´m not the jealous guy."

I was already trying to get rid of the tears in my eyes, but he noticed them, he sighed lightly and moved me around to face me.

The sheets didn´t work with me and fell back on the bed, something he appreciated because his hands moved towards my body, caressing my jawline down to my chest, my already aroused breasts before placing both hands on either side of my waist moving me towards him. He kissed me, pressed me against him and finally we fell together backwards. He pulled up the sheets over us and chuckled a little, as his body formed after mine.

I was packing up the last box of fruit during the afternoon, but I couldn´t stop thinking about how the afternoon siesta had become an afternoon of love and sex between us. A smile and suddenly Gabriel was right there, sniffing my neck, whispering "I know what you´re thinking, I was thinking about that too. Do you think, um, we could, um repeat that tonight after dinner?" Those chills along my spine again, I closed my eyes and his hands travelled along my arms, wrapping me in. "Mm…nothing would make me happier, but I have to go home to grams. We´re together a lot here and I don´t have much time with her but trust me, I would love to stay. Can we do this some other time?" I said and moved around to face him.

He made space so I could stay wrapped in his arms, my head underneath his chin and I could hear his heart beating slowly, almost seducing me into sleep. "Maybe tomorrow? Around siesta time? Or even now, we don´t have any customers and it´s almost 7 pm." I raised my eyebrows, suddenly my tired face wasn´t tired anymore even though my brain was still adjusting to the light. Gabriel smirked, kissed my head and then my lips, saying "Tomorrow would be great, that will give you time to miss me a little." Now, get ready and I´ll give you a ride home." I sighed and went to pick up my bag, grabbed the helmet while he locked in the cash in the tiny safe. He then locked the doors and turned on the alarm, I put on the helmet, and we rode off in his motorcycle.

At grandma´s house, we kissed goodnight and said our goodbyes. She was watching tv in her bedroom when I sneaked in my head "Hey grams, I´m home. What are you watching?" She moved a little and I sat beside her, there was this cheesy novella on tv. I remembered watching a lot of those when I was younger, but nowadays it just didn´t go with me. "Do you want me to make you a snack?" she said, and I smiled "No thanks grams, I can fix it. Would you like something?" She had a tray beside her, apparently, she already had some so I gave her a quick hug and went to the kitchen. A shadow was lurking around the patio, so I grabbed the closest wooden spatula and went out, hit him hard over the head and turned on the lights. It was Gabriel. "What the hell are you doing here? I could've killed you!! How did you get in?" I said and checked his head, he was laughing at the same time as petting my grandma's dog. "Sorry, I thought that I could make you see me but instead you hit me on the head. Is your grandma asleep? I thought I could spend the night here, no funny business just you know, cuddle."

I blushed, I never had a guy over at grams, not even back home with my mom and sister in the same house. We sneaked back in, and I checked grams bedroom to see if she was asleep, when it was clear, we went to my room and closed the door. Gabriel held me in his arms for a while before sitting and making himself comfortable in my childhood bed, I went out to get a t-shirt from my uncle's pile in the laundry room and a pair of trainers that belonged to my late grandfather. Everything fit him perfectly (of course I watched him undress and change, what did you think?) and he sat right beside me on the bed. His stomach and mine growled, so I went to the kitchen to fix a snack for us.

I didn´t want to warm up anything because the microwave made too much noise so it would have to be sandwiches and tea.

"What´s taking so long?" he said and was about to start laughing because I dropped the bread on the floor, within seconds I grabbed it and said, "5 second rule". He pulled my t-shirt, so I moved closer to him, and he sniffed my neck, giggled a little and said, "I love you." That had to be the first time he said it in words, because actions speak louder than words and I must say that this time it felt deep within me that he truly meant it. He smiled, his cheeks were pinkish and this shy look on his face. I touched his cheek and whispered, "Come on, let´s go back to my room and finish this snack."

TWELVE

SEVILLAN CHRISTMAS

Christmas time and Sevilla is quite beautiful with its lights and ornaments in every corner. I was on my way to pick up my mom and sister at the airport in the car with Gabriel, it´s the first time they´re going to meet and I hope they´re on their best behavior *pause for laughter*. Fidgety and nervous I looked out the window, Gabriel met my eyes in the mirror in front and said "Relax, everything will be alright, and I hope your family likes me. Besides, in the end everything that counts it´s if you like me. Right? You do like me?" I couldn´t hold my laughter, he´s right, if we ever get married it will be us two but isn´t it like an unwritten rule that you also marry the family?

At the airport we noticed that the plane from Barcelona was a bit delayed, so we had some coffee and tea for me while we waited.

Gabriel put his arm around me, kissed my head and held my cold hands for me to get warm.

The tea wasn´t really doing its job and suddenly a text from mom "We´ve arrived, going for the luggage and we´ll see you soon!". We walked towards baggage claim, and I saw a familiar face…my mom. "Momma!!!!" I yelled and ran to her; she was thrilled to see me and then I saw Mary. This had to be the longest we´ve been apart because last time we saw each other was over 6 months ago. She was crying when she saw me, I hugged her tight and said, "Stop crying silly, you´re here now." I took the luggage and put it on the cart that Gabriel had brought over, so this was the best time to present him "Mom, sis, this is Gabriel my boyfriend. Gabriel, this is the other half of my family: My mom Gianna and my sister Mary." He smiled towards them, stretched out his hand to salute them. Mom took his hand, then Mary and they smiled towards me "Well, you found a good guy. How did you meet?" I opened my eyes wide, and Gabriel laughed a little "Well Mrs. Gianna, we met ages ago outside the same school where Grace went. I worked in the tiny kiosk with my grandfather, selling candy and other snacks to the schoolkids." Mom thought for a while, he seemed familiar to her, but she only dropped me off to school once or twice while we lived in Sevilla. "Oh yes, I think I remember you. What do you do for a living?" she continued, and he explained his fruit/vegetables business that now was doing online deliveries with my help. "It was Grace's idea to expand my business, she's in charge of the online orders and deliveries. She's very bright and I love her." He said and my mom almost choked, apart from the disaster Perry caused in my life she thought I would never date again and now he was telling them that he loved me.

I sat in front with him, mom, and sis in the backseat. Everything went well and now we were surprising grams with their visit, she didn't know that they were staying with us for Christmas. I opened the gate to her house as Gabriel parked the car and told her I had an early gift for her, she came to the door and almost fell to the ground when she saw mom and Mary. They cried, happy to see each other again and helped them in with the bags. When she saw Gabriel, she gave him a hug and said "Oh kind boy, come in, come in." Grams made a great dinner for us; we were all very hungry after the ride to the airport and back.

I went to my room to get the camera for a family picture and suddenly Gabriel was right there "Hey, your family is nice.

I´m glad they like me, for a moment I thought that she was going to hate me because of the fruit/vegetable business but no, she´s really chill.

This is going very well, don´t you think? Maybe now you can spend the night at my place, your grams got company." I turned around to hug him and he was more than happy to keep me in his arms, a quick kiss before we went back to the kitchen.

After dinner, mom and sis went to bed, grams did the same and only Gabriel, and I were awake in the yard with the dog. He had his hand on my hair, scratching lightly and I fell asleep towards his chest, listening to the birds chirping and his drumming heartbeat. Suddenly he said, "We should get married, I think your mom would be very relaxed to know that her daughter is taken care of, would you?" I couldn´t hear him clearly or wasn´t sure that I heard him right. "What?" I said and sat up a little. He put his cheek next to mine and the heat from it warmed me from the chilly afternoon "I said, would you marry me?" I tried to stay awake for a while, unsure if I had heard right or not. "Is it not a bit sudden? We´ve been together for almost a year, do you think we´re ready?"

He sighed, put the hand in his pocket and took out a bag of candy pacifiers, offered me one and said, "When I can get you a proper ring, I will but for now think you could accept this?" I took it, put it on my finger and then ate it. Gabriel laughed and we kissed, I guess we´re now engaged.

I wrapped the last gifts for the family and kept them at Gabriel´s apartment, his gift I kept at grams house and that one I bought a long time ago. He had told me that he wanted to buy a new watch, a Swatch that he had seen on tv. I checked the price and it wasn´t much so I got it for him, other than that I got him a shirt and a sweater, I think some aftershave too. He had just closed the shop for the weekend and tomorrow we would only work until 1 pm so we were both relaxed. I don´t know if it was his sweaty face and t-shirt that turned me on but as soon as he entered the room, I threw myself in his arms. "Hey there missy, what ´cha doing?" he said and grabbed a hold on me, gave me a kiss and was about to let me go when I locked my lips on his. He did try to talk but I wouldn´t let him, so he just gave up. I unbuttoned his shirt, and he realized what I was about to do, he smiled through our kiss and lifted my shirt, continued to unbutton my jeans.

He kissed my neck, our breaths were getting stronger by the minute, as I pulled off his pants, I saw that he couldn´t wait much longer. We moved towards the couch, and he pinned me underneath him as he entered me first carefully and then with full strength. It was delicate, sexy, and tired, while I rested on his chest, and he wrapped the blanket around us. He could barely breathe when he said "Wow, I didn´t know that you were so in need for me today. Should´ve come in sooner, I was doing some inventory." We kissed, got dressed and I said, "During lunch, I sent a text to mom that I wouldn´t come home tonight so we could stay at your place." He beamed, normally I didn´t stay the whole night but now we could finally spend the night before Christmas together and tomorrow tell my family that we were engaged. After closing, we went to the grocery store around the corner to buy some beef and rice for tonight's dinner. The vegetables were already picked from his store so no need to buy something else, I had this small cart with me, and he walked by my side.

At times I caught him admiring me from a short distance and when he saw me, he smiled big.

At Gabriel's I was doing some dishes and he was cutting up the tomatoes, the beef was cooking in the oven along with the veggies. It smelled fantastic and he stole a kiss or two in between. We ate in silence, he seemed worried, so I asked "Hey, are you okay?" He gave me a weak smile and nodded "Everything is just fine, don't worry." But I didn't let it go "You know you can tell me anything, right? What's on your mind?" He smirked, looked slightly happier now and got up, grabbed my hands and said "I need you, let's just leave everything here and go to bed. I'll do the dishes later, just be with me." We went to the bedroom and laid there, side by side, looking at the sunlight in the ceiling. I still didn't understand why he was so worried, so I tried again "Are you going to tell me what's going on?" He sighed, turned to my side and whispered "I keep thinking why you're at my side, working with me, making me happy, allowing your family to get to know me and loving me. I didn't think it would be possible to find love, considering my own parents left and then my grandfather. If you ever left, I don't think I could bear it, I would probably die."

Tears in his eyes, now I understood: He thought he couldn't keep love to him because of what had happened so early in his life, maybe thinking that he didn't deserve it or something. My eyes filled with tears as well, I cupped my hands around his wet face and kissed him gently. He smiled in between, looked more restored and I felt his sad desperation turn into a more carnal one as his kisses switched from sweet and innocent to fiercely leaving me out of breath.

"Do you want to have kids? I know we never talked about this before and I hope that it's not a dealbreaker, I guess the whole idea for me is to have what I didn't have before you know." He said and held me tight in his strong arms, I sighed, it was true, we never talked about kids before and considering I was in an age that's far too old to have children maybe he needed someone younger, with the possibility. To be honest was the best thing to do, so I did "Gabriel, I can't have kids. A long time ago, I did a check-up at the doctors, and he told me that one of my tubes is practically non existing. If you want to have kids, don't want to adopt, maybe you need another girlfriend. Someone younger that can give you what I can´t."

I got up from the bed, just sat there by the edge of it and tried to hide my tears from him.

It didn´t take long before he wrapped his arms around me and said "I didn´t say that it had to be our blood, I would welcome any child as long as we welcome it together. Even if you didn´t carry him or her for 9 months, I still want it to have you as their mother." I smiled weakly, I didn´t have to look into his eyes to know that he was telling the truth. "How come that you don´t care as long as we adopt together? I thought all guys wanted their children, not others." I said and pulled my back to his chest, he kissed my cheek and comforted me, holding on to my hands "Not all guys are fitted to be fathers, but I would make it my lives goal to be the best father to our child and you know why?" I think I knew but still wanted him to tell me "No, why?" He whispered, "Because I love you and that child is yours, for that I can´t do anything but love it with all my heart."

Christmas eve in the morning, we were getting ready for the dinner at grams house and my nerves were playing with my mind all day.

Gabriel had been weird, looking over his shoulder, checking his phone and for a moment it would seem like he was flirting with every female customer. Since I didn´t work with him outside I barely saw him but today, when I finally peeked, I realized that he was being flirty. I wasn´t the jealous type, I never cared when guys flirted because I knew myself too well to continue their jokes. But now, it was different, I was becoming insecure just by looking at him being overly friendly. I stayed calm, he didn´t check in with me during his break and now I was furious.

By closing time, around 2 pm, he was already wearing his helmet and said "I got to do a thing, do you mind going home by yourself? I´ll be at your grandmas in time, okay? Love you, bye." I didn´t say anything back, too busy being grumpy girlfriend as I muttered the final orders and closing the computer.

He had a fancy shirt in the closet by the door and I really needed to smell his scent, normally he didn´t leave without giving me a kiss but like I said, he was sketchy all day long. In one of the pockets, I found a receipt for flowers, the address wasn´t nearby so I checked in my phone. It was a house in the center of Sevilla, owned by a Catalina Salas. No other name registered in her home, so I guess she lived alone, when I saw her age, my jaw dropped: 25 years old. The bastard was cheating! Instead of tears, my anger rose to the surface and my mind went black. I closed the door to the store; he could fix his own delivery schedule because I was done with him. Really done.

Furious I went home to my grams, they were all happy decorating, and my heart was devastated to know that Gabriel, the guy I was loving so much and making plans was cheating on me with a 25-year-old. Mom saw my angry face and came to my room "Hey, you, okay? What´s with the angry face?" She sat next to me on the bed, I barely got a word out and began crying "He´s cheating on me!!!" Mom looked surprised but said "Did you catch him?" I looked at her and showed her the receipt (I kept it just in case he threw it away and called me a loon), but still, she didn´t tell me to end things with him. She was unusually calm... Did she know something I didn't? "Mom, you don´t look very surprised. Do you know something about this?"

She sighed, then spilled the beans "I´m sorry honey, I tried to tell you but yesterday you didn´t come home but yes.

He is cheating and this girl, I know her. Her grandmother is our old neighbor, Mrs. Salas." I could barely keep it together, mom comforted me, and I said "I want to go back to Barcelona, after Christmas mom. I´ll find a new job and…" The tears overflowed my eyes and I couldn´t do anything else but cry in her arms.

I woke up in my own bed, had lost track of time but checked the old clock on the wall: 8 pm. There were voices coming from the kitchen, laughter, jokes coming and going. I got up and stapled out of my room towards the noise "Mom?" Everyone was there: mom, sister, grams, uncle, his girlfriend, and Gabriel. My confused head couldn´t understand and suddenly they said, "Merry Christmas!!" I still didn´t get it but Gabriel came towards me and said, "To think you almost ruined the surprise, come on sleepy head, I have something for you."

In grams little living room, apart from the Christmas tree there was a huge bouquet of flowers and a medium box, like from the jewelers.

Confused I went with him to see it, he put his arms around me and said, "This is for you, Merry Christmas, I really hope you like it because I chose it especially for you." I scratched my eyes, more awake now and opened the box: it was a necklace in white gold with a heart in rosé gold. It was beautiful and delicate, but I didn´t understand...why would he buy something like this if he was cheating? I turned to him, and he whispered, so quietly I could barely hear him "I would never cheat, lie nor hurt you." He helped me with the necklace and suddenly he was on his knees, with another box "And this, goes with the necklace and with the next question... Graciela, would you do me the honor to be my life companion, love of my life and mother of our children?" In his teary eyes I found out the truth: he loved me. My family were all staring at us, he stayed on his knees and I...I fainted.

"Honey, you´re awake. Are you okay?" mom said and checked my blood pressure, I looked around me but there were only us two in the room. "Yeah mom, I´m fine. Just dizzy, wait, did I just dream all that?" For a moment it felt like none of it had happened but then I saw Gabriel peeking in through the door "Hey, can I come in?" Mom gave him a smile and said, "Come in, I´ll check in on you later or you can just join us for dinner." He smiled and gave her a hug, said something to her that I didn´t hear and came to sit next to me.

"I hope this isn´t a no from you, because we´re engaged in secret, remember the pacifier ring?" he said and gave me a big smile, I smiled back but felt the need to ask, "What about the receipt I found?" Gabriel seemed confused but then said "She´s my best friend, I asked her to keep the flowers at her house so you wouldn´t know. Your mom helped me out with that since they know each other, oh and she´s married you know. I don´t have many people to rely on so I turned to your family, they helped me to make the best Christmas for you because normally you make it for them. Oh, and this, belongs to you." He stroked my hair and showed me the ring, the one he had told me the day before was on its way. I smiled weakly, I had just let my jealousy get the best of me and doubted the one person that only withheld information to make me happy. "Thank you and yes, I´ll marry you." I said and he pressed his forehead against mine before putting it on me. We hugged, kissed and he walked me through the door towards the family already eating and he yelled "She said YES!!!" They cheered and came up to congratulate us, although I already said yes, the day before to him in private, I realized that it was equally important to have the family have a moment like this.

We sat down by the table and Gabriel said "I would like to say a few words before we continue this marvelous feast. First, thank you for receiving me in your home as a future family member but also because you made me feel welcome. I didn´t have the possibility to have a family and was almost raised entirely by my grandfather, God rest his soul, and now I want to raise my own family with Grace. Cheers to you and to my future wife, I love you." My family was overwhelmed by his words and so was I, but was I ready to get married?

THIRTEEN

"ENGAGED, NO MORE"

I looked at the ring on my finger, it looked like it
belonged there but somehow, I thought that
maybe it was too soon. If Gabriel was the one,
how come it felt so strange to be called fiancée by
him? Our first night after Christmas was very
strange, my whole family was sleeping under the
same roof and we couldn´t exactly make too
much noise. He was incredibly turned on and I,
well I couldn´t stay put so, we tried to keep it as
quiet as possible by turning on the tv with some
boring game show but it didn´t work. Instead, we
talked about how this whole marriage thing would
work: we were engaged, we would marry in
Sevilla, stay here with the shop and everything.
Which sounds like a great idea, my family wasn´t
that big and I didn´t have that many friends to
invite so it would be a very intimate party.

I wrote down everything we could need, and Gabriel agreed to everything, which is a good sign since arguing about the wedding and the reception shouldn´t be the first thing you do the first days.

Running through the airport with about 15 minutes before the gate closed was like running through a mall looking for the exit. I wasn´t that happy to travel because it meant that I could run into Perry while being there but hopefully, he would be too busy to notice. Gabriel drove us to the airport, since I was also leaving mom and sis back in Barcelona, but they would come back for the wedding plans in February. They had to try the dresses, nothing fancy but still a treat from me to them but the real treat was the shoes: Gucci flats. We 3 sat by the window, with me by the aisle and there was some strange feeling about going back. It felt like it wasn´t my home anymore and I told mom this, that maybe they should consider moving here closer to both grams and me. Mom said that they would think about it but usually that means that she doesn´t want to, I knew her far too well. We arrived in Barcelona about 2 hours later, I remembered when I went to this convention ages ago and it was so much fun. Everything was less of a problem back then.

Mom´s house was different since I moved to Sevilla, my old stuff was still in their places and for a moment I was back to be that girl again.

A text from Gabriel woke me up from memory lane "Hey, how was the flight? Can I call you later? I miss you already, love you. XOXO G" I sent him a picture back "Everything is fine, please do, missing you too. Won´t be here too long, just going to see my friends and invite them to the wedding. Won´t be getting cards lol XD. Call me around 7 pm, maybe we could do something through the phone hint hint XOXX".

I decided to meet up my friends at work, it´s been a long time since I last saw them, but it would be enough to wait by the entrance. Don´t want to run into unpleasant people as well. While sitting on the bench closest to the window, I saw 2 people coming from the elevator and to my big surprise it was Perry and Natalie. The sworn enemies became lovers after all, he carried her bag, and she was big over the belly… she was pregnant! Luckily, they didn´t look at me but I was appalled to see them *happy together*. A few minutes after they left, my friends arrived happy to see me, but I couldn't get the image out of my head: Perry was in love with her, despite that he denied it when we were standing right here trying to defend our love from her. He's such a liar!

"We're so happy for you, what's he like? I thought you would never date again Perry, but did you know that it took him 2 seconds to move on?" That's all I heard all the way to the restaurant and the anger in my heart just grew stronger by the minute, but not because I saw them together but how my own friends kept going on and on about it. "Listen guys, guys, now that's enough! I'm an engaged woman, trying to tell you that you're invited to the wedding and you just keep talking about them. I honestly don't care what they do together, Perry visited me in Sevilla, and I told him to get lost. I love Gabriel, he loves me and he doesn't have any attachments to other women. If you're interested, the wedding is in 2 months from now. If not, that's okay too." I said and got up, leaving quickly, calling Gabriel "Hey baby, I was just thinking about you. Slow down, slow down, I don't understand. 2 months, sure, I don't mind. Coming home tomorrow? What about your family?" he said, and I rambled on. I had to sit in the park for a while to catch my breath and he could hear me better "Hey, I know things are being tough there but see it this way: I'll pick you up myself from Barcelona tomorrow in the afternoon. I´m taking the bike, we could stop on the way and have fun together.

Give me your address, okay, writing it down so I´ll see you tomorrow. What? Oh yeah of course when you get home. Yes, yes, I´ll check with you first. Okay honey, talk soon. Love you, bye." I stayed in the park for a while, it took some energy to calm down and to realize that maybe they weren´t my friends.

When I came home to my mother´s, she said that dinner was ready and come to think of it I hadn´t eaten all day. Evening came and I went to my old bedroom, closed the door, changed clothes, and called Gabriel, video call. He looked so good in his white t-shirt, I could see his chest underneath (Thank God for see through white t-shirts) and I think he knew that I could see because he kept stretching towards the ceiling. He was worried about me, so I told him the truth: that I saw my ex with my ex-boss and that it bothered me, not because they were an item but that he lied about it. He could´ve just told me the truth instead of coming up with these stupid lies about that he needed to be engaged with her because of his father etc. etc. Gabriel said "Whoa, slow down girlie. As far as I know, the dude came here to

Sevilla to talk and you guys did that, you blew him off, basically told him to get lost. Tell me, the truth, do you still love him?" I was numb, what if he was right? Did I still love Perry, even though he had told me a bunch of lies? If that was true, what did I feel for Gabriel? He stayed in vision but looked sad, I think he knew the answer to that "Maybe you need some distance, to think things through. I´ll be here whenever you need me, but you need to take the decision to stay or go, I would never ask you to stay if I knew that you´re unsure. Take care of yourself honey." He hung up and I couldn´t say anything more, I had nothing on my mind.

I put the phone on the bedside table and stared at the ceiling, slowly I faded into deep sleep with nothing on my mind except: I think I´ve just been dumped.

Weeks later (still nothing from Gabriel, nor my friends but that was my choice) I was still at mom´s, called grams once a week (I think she realized that the engagement had been called off) and I sent a FedEx to Gabriel with the ring inside, a note that I was sorry but maybe this was the best for both of us.

He understood, told me to do what my heart truly wanted but the truth was that none of them were important anymore, just a chapter in my life.

Even though I was almost 42 now, I felt more secure about staying alone rather than having someone just to avoid being alone.

I was reading in the afternoon´s remaining sunlight when mom popped in her head and said, "Can we talk?". I nodded, put down the book on the bed and sat up. She sat next to me, with her little smile and reminded me of when I was little, when she needed to tell me something difficult. "I´m sensing that you and Gabriel will no longer continue working together, since you barely talk to each other. Did you dissolve the society you both had?" Great, she wanted to discuss business rather than feelings. I sighed heavily "We did, I signed over everything to him and he suggested that we could divide the money, but I said no. It would be unfair to him if I wanted to keep it to myself, but yeah he did give me something." Mom looked confused, I smiled within because even if Gabriel and I didn´t end up together we could still be civil people talking about things that didn´t involve love. Well, she didn´t know that we hadn´t talked since the FedEx delivery and frankly she didn't have to know everything. "What are your plans now?

Will you stay here, find a new job or maybe you want to see the world?" she said, and I had already a plan in mind, no it didn't involve getting Perry back because I realized that I didn't need a man in my life to feel complete, I just needed me. I smiled and patted mom on her hand that was resting on her leg "Mom, don't you worry. I have a plan and many ideas; one will surely stick to me and work." She looked calmer now and I had time to think things over a little more.

6 MONTHS LATER

I finally started my own company, as an interior decorator. With my grades, curriculum and experience it didn't take long to build it up from the ground: an office in central Barcelona, a part time receptionist that worked with bookings, phone calls and emails from the patients o and patients that had heard about the new place. My office wasn't close to my old job, it wasn't close to Perry's apartment (although I had received info from a friend at my old job that he quit and moved from Barcelona), so I felt pleased to reinvent my life.

Funny how I didn´t miss the men in my life, I just felt so comfortable with myself again.

Maybe that´s why I had doubts, because I realized that I don´t need a man to do whatever I want with my life.

FOURTEEN

EDINBURGH IN MY HEART

At last, a time for myself and what better than to travel again, this time to Scotland. I said bye to mom and sister early in the morning before taking the subway to the airport, to wait for the plane to Edinburgh. Since I was little, I wanted to visit, not only because I saw "Braveheart" but also for its nature and castles.

I saw a guy park his motorcycle outside the airport and my heart skipped a beat, but when he took off his helmet, I saw that it wasn´t Gabriel. Somehow, I keep thinking about him coming, not on a horse, but a bike to rescue me even though I don´t need rescuing from anything nor anyone. With passport and ticket in hand, I passed through security and waited by the gate, to then enter the plane. Edinburgh awaits. 2 hours later the plane was landing in their airport, I barely understood their accents, but I kept thinking in my mind that

William Wallace would probably be an airport security executive checking passports. Plane parked, people in a rush to get out and I stayed put until half of them got off, got my carry-on, and got off. The airport was big, they had some typical Scottish tartans, satchels, kilts, and different foods. I knew I needed to stay away from the haggis, based entirely on entrails and whatnot *eurgh*. Checking the way to the airport coach that took me to town, to find my hotel Britannia, something budget was always nice. I bought my ticket, waited for my turn to be seated and the chauffeur said, "Where to lassie?" I told him to town center, and he showed me to my seat, I put on my seatbelt and waited for departure. The air felt adventurous, this well needed vacation was my first on my own since the split and I couldn´t wait to see what was waiting for me.

At last, in my hotel room, very simple which suited me very well. Quick shower and change clothes to see the town, I always use my time to the limit since time literally flies away. The town is old, the smell of fresh rain on the stones that marked every road to and from the city. It´s people, both natives and tourists walking around mostly happy, me marveling at every building, it´s constructions and giving me ideas for my job. So more than a simple vacation, this was research. Before I entered a nice and homely bar around the corner from my hotel, I saw a man on a bike drive by, there was my heart again dreaming that Gabriel was here close to me. "What would you like to drink lassie?" the old man at the counter said, since I didn't drink alcohol it felt weird to ask for it, but I just said, "Do you have any iced tea?" He looked like I was crazy but then a man said, "She don't do alcohol mate, give her the tea." I turned around, there was Gabriel. Before he came closer, I pinched myself in the arm because I could swear that he wasn't here. My legs tingled, he looked so handsome and I wasn't sure how I would stay away from his arms that apparently my body missed. He was right by me side and just passed directly to the man at the bar. The pitcher of tea, two glasses and he winked at me "Come on lass, we have a lot to talk about." I followed him as he chose a table in the corner, we could barely hear each other in the noise but his eyes searched for mine. I sat down in front of him, still appalled by having him so close to me that I didn't know what to say. But he did, luckily, otherwise awkward silence. "So, you're here in Scotland all alone. Why?"

Sometimes he was brute when he spoke, almost like he was mad at me, like he was a teacher and wanted to punish me.

"I…" I began and stopped; it was like I was ashamed to let move on with my life without Perry and him. He looked at me, his eyes smiled through his serious face and then it was the serious hand grabbing "I miss you and I came here to beg you to take me back." I didn´t move my hand, I didn´t say anything, I just sat there frozen by his words. The hand grabbing turned into a soft touch, each finger had extra fingers that held them tight, and he suppressed a smile. With my free hand I pulled his shirt from across the table and planted a kiss on his warm lips, his hand that was interlocked with mine suddenly appeared on my cheeks, holding me and continued that kiss. The table was in the way, and he passed around to my side, getting a tight grip on my waist and I put my arm around his neck. Gabriel smiled in between, he couldn´t hide it anymore and neither could I, but could we make it work? What was so different now?

He let me go slowly, sat me down and he kneeled in front of me "I´m sorry, I couldn´t help it but I´ve missed you.

Your touch, your lips, your smell, you´re everything to me. If you look me in the eyes and say that you don´t, feel anything, I´ll walk away. No remorse, no more tries. Just tell me." I looked around me, people were too busy in their business and the world was just pulling us two together. "Where are you staying?" I said, because I didn´t have a direct answer and maybe now would be too rash to tell him no. He moved closer to my ear and whispered "Why, are you trying to get me to bed lassie?" in a perfect Scottish accent and then spoke normally "At the Thistle, you?" I couldn´t hold my laughter "The Britannia" which was very budget but not as bad as a hostel where you share rooms with 10 others. His eyes were on fire, I knew what he was thinking and I wasn´t even there, maybe a little snogging, shirtless preferably. *OMG* I was blushing now, and he understood that whatever he wanted to do tonight was going his way, hopefully if something happened tonight it wouldn´t be just a one-night stand.

 Gabriel finished his glass of tea, and I was still on half, he stood up and said "I´m going to pay for the tea, then we could uh, finish the conversation at the Thistle. If you like."

He winked, went to the counter, and paid the man, they whispered something, and he patted his arm. I finished my tea slowly and went to the counter to ask what was said, the man smiled at me and said, "I hope you work this out lassie, that is a good man out there and he loves you to pieces...He told me that you were his wife, or at least he wanted you to be." I smiled at him; my face was burning up and I needed to see where this would end. I walked through the crowd and got out; Gabriel was standing in a corner against the wall with his helmet in hand. I walked over to him, and he said, "So you´re still curious about me then, admit it." There was cockiness in his voice, I didn´t want to give him that satisfaction so I responded "No, I´m not curious. In fact, I´m walking to my hotel so I guess I´ll see you. Goodnight, thanks for the tea." I turned around, put on my jacket, and walked in normal tact towards my hotel when he came running from behind me, pulled my jacket so I turned over and almost lost my balance. He grabbed my waist again, held it tight so I couldn´t move and he kissed me "Damn it woman, I can´t let you walk into the night like this." Now it was my turn to laugh, and he shushed me with another kiss, this one was not tender and sweet.

"Are you trying to seduce me sir?" I said and he pulled me away (not too much but enough to look me in the eyes). "No, I´m trying to get you to marry me because I love you. Forget the past, what you and I have is real, it doesn't get any more real than this. If you didn´t love me back, why did you let me kiss you?" I pouted, it´s not like I had a choice but then again, I liked his kisses, tender or not. It´s true, I did miss him, I saw him everywhere, but it was long after we split. Was fate trying to tell me he was the one?

"Did I lose you to space or still here?" he teased, and I pressed my nose to his chest, he caressed the back of my head moving away my hair that was in the way of my neck. His breath was calm, I could hear his heartbeats and I didn´t want to let him go. "I´m here." I whispered and he held me tighter, now he was staring at my forehead, waiting for me to look up. "So, do you want me to come over to your budget place or do you want to take advantage of the Thistle with me included?" I could see his smile, without even looking I pressed my lips towards his but since I was shorter than him, the kiss ended on his chin. "Ahh my bonnie lass." He said and pulled me up in his arms, now we were equally tall, and he leaned in for a kiss.

"So, care to take a bike ride to the Thistle or shall we stay here tonight and maybe move over the tomorrow?" He put me down and I thought for a moment "The Thistle sounds great, but I need to get some stuff from my bags." He wrinkled his forehead and said with a cheeky voice "Unless you want to spend the rest of the evening naked, I do have sheets you can wear." I laughed, it did sound kind of funny, so I grabbed his arm "Fine, let´s go." I sat behind him on his bike, helmet on and we rode off into the night.

The Thistle was not what I expected: antique like outside, inside was almost like being at the opera with chandeliers and that hideous wallpaper *pause for laughter*. The night manager raised an eyebrow towards us, and Gabriel let me go, went up to him and said something that I didn´t get. The man nodded and he came right back to me smiling, whispered "I was just telling him that you were my woman for the night and that we did not want to be disturbed." I widened my eyes, looking shameful at the man and he was smiling "I hope you didn´t mean that, what´s he going to think?" I said, feeling the shame rising to my cheeks turning them red. He whispered as we walked up the stairs "Actually, I think he said that I got myself quite the catch. Oh, and he´s bringing us some food later, I´m hungry as a horse. You?" Outside his room, he opened the door, and it was beautiful: a big bed, older cupboards, and his bag on the floor. I went in and he behind me, closing the door and suddenly grabbed my waist. "How can you compare the Britannia to this? Is your bed even this comfy?" He ran towards it with me in his arms, I tripped and fell right into it with him underneath me "Careful, I´m going to break your ribs like this." I shouted and he snuggled into my face. Gabriel caressed away a lock of hair on my face and breathed so close that I could feel his lips towards mine, I closed my eyes thinking that this could be one of those dreams but when I opened them again, he was still there.

"I´m here, right here with you and even if you tell me to go I wouldn´t. You´re my prisoner or is it the other way around?" he said, and his nose pressed against mine, I leaned my lips towards his, meeting in the middle of us both.

Someone knocked on the door and he smiled "That has to be the haggis." I really hoped not because of what I read on it, it wouldn´t be nice to even smell it. "Hey, thank you so much man. Here, no disturbances until tomorrow yeah?"

A small cart with food and a pitcher of iced tea, that smelt delicious. "Hungry honey?" he asked and opened the serving dishes: grilled meats, cold cuts, pasta, and buttered potatoes. By the smell only I realized how hungry I really was, we sat in the middle of the bed, plate in hands and smiled towards each other. After the late-night supper, we cuddled in bed, still fully clothed and listened to music from his phone. He was sitting behind me, his arms folded over mine holding me tight and his cheek touching mine as he was humming "Galway Girl", Irish folk song even though weren´t in Galway.

"There´s something we need to talk about, I sold the company and I moved here. Well, I just arrived 2 days before you did and went to see the man from the bar about an apartment when I saw you. I got a job at his bar too, so I thought if you wanted to join me or are you going back to Barcelona?" I couldn´t imagine his little shop without him, I couldn´t imagine being there knowing he´s not even in the same country but I just started this company and I couldn´t leave everything to be near him. Or could I? I sat quiet with him still holding on to me, both thinking how we could make this work or if we even should try it out. Gabriel noticed my worried face and he kissed my cheek "We don't have to decide yet, I mean you're still here and how long are you staying?" I turned my face towards his lips, feeling his breath and said, "Tonight or in general?"

He chuckled, "In general of course. I know you're staying with me until you need to go back, that reminds me, tomorrow you must check out from your budget hotel and stay here. I'll clear it with the manager, don't you worry." I sighed and he squeezed me tighter, then he saw the tears "But, why are you crying? Did I say something?" I nodded my head, "I'm not worried about staying here, with you. I'm thinking about what my family will say about me moving here, with you." I almost fell backwards when he moved away to face me, happy and thrilled he hugged me, we kissed, and he said "Is it true? Are you staying?" I nodded again, I knew that he was the one I wanted to keep in my life and was it so bad to live in Edinburgh? Not really, it was 2 hours from Barcelona, we would travel there to see my family and they could come here. I mean mom always wanted to visit Edinburgh; it would be the perfect reason. "Yes, I want to stay with you for my journey and then I'll go back to gather my stuff, but how big is your apartment? Will it be enough for us?" I said and he was also rather emotional

"We´ll go tomorrow after we move your things, I won´t be able to accompany you back to Barcelona but I´ll ask a friend. He has this big truck and travels through Calais to London, drive the extra miles here with your things. You won´t need to pay anything, I´ll sort it out. Jorje likes his English beer, so I´ll buy him a barrel ha-ha. Oh babe, this will be great. You and me, we´ll be good!" He took me in his arms, held me tight and kissed me. I thought about moving my company here, then I needed to call off the lease on the office and sack my employee but maybe I could do something about that.

I had a friend that worked at the DMV, and they needed someone part time, so maybe my assistant could go there, personal note to ring her in the morning.

"Hey, no work. Want to dance?" he said, got out of the bed and stretched out his hand to me. I took it and he swung me around, pressed the phone on the table to Spotify, he had this playlist named "US", put it on "Random" and we danced to the first song that came up "Set adrift on memory bliss". Odd since we weren´t on a desert island but it worked, I wasn´t much of a dancer but luckily, he was. I just followed his footsteps.

FIFTEEN

A TEARFUL GOODBYE

Edinburgh had been marvelous, full of mystery and good food (nope still a big no on the haggis, no offence to the Scots but no). Well, Gabriel was also marvelous and loving but now it was time for me to travel back to Barcelona and tell my family that I was moving to Gabriel´s in Edinburgh. We stood at the airport, 3 hours before my flight departure and I was already crying because it would take some time before we would see each other again. He held me in his arms, tightly, his motorcycle helmet was on the floor and my bag was already checked in, so I was only bringing my backpack with me "I´ll call you tonight when you´re home okay? But send me a text when you land, so I can be calm because I won´t be until you´re back with me, like this. I love you Grace, and I´ll wait for you. Safe travels." His words touched my soul, I didn´t want to leave him like this but I knew I needed to do a lot of things before being able to move that far away.

I stood on my toes, to be able to kiss his eyelids, then his cheeks to finally kiss his lips that tasted salty from his tears. Now I was crying too, not ugly cry like I normally do but you know lots of tears, he dried my face with the palm of his hand, and I took it in mine to kiss it too.

The airport callback "Flight 343 to Barcelona, boarding starts in 30 minutes."

"Time to go, I´ll call or text as soon as I land. Take care of yourself, okay? I love you." I said and left him there, standing amongst other people saying goodbye to their loved ones. Passing through security, gave the police my passport and ticket for check-up, went through the metal detector and something beeped. I checked my pockets and found a little pouch, opened it quickly and noticed a simple ring with a paper note "Wear this until you come back to me, then choose if you want to marry me or not. Love you always, Gabriel XXX" I looked surprised at the officer, and she smiled, I passed the detector again and it didn´t beep so now I gathered my things, putting on the ring on my left finger.

"Bienvenidos al aeropuerto El Prat de Barcelona, por favor mantenga su asiento hasta que el avión haya aparcado en el terminal. Gracias." I woke up from my very short nap, it was now 6 pm and since Edinburgh is one hour behind, it was 5 pm there. I wondered what Gabriel was doing now, probably working at the bar or maybe home. Home, what a weird sense to have a home in another place so far away from your family too. The same family was waiting at the baggage claim, we hugged and cried a little, when Mary noticed the ring "You got married????!!!!" Shit.... explain.

"Well not exactly but I got a proposal on a piece of paper at the airport." I said and mom wrinkled her nose in excitement, but then her face was all serious "From who?" I smiled and said "Well, from Gabriel. He went to Edinburgh, and we met in a bar, he had been following me since I got there and while talking, I realized that he´s the one mom. He got a job there, an apartment and he loves me, we talked about moving in together."

And there it was, the news that I was so afraid of telling my family: I wanted to live with Gabriel in Edinburgh.

I have no idea how it was going to work out, but I did want to try, he was the only one that truly wanted me in his life and didn´t want to lose me.

While talking to my family I remembered that I had totally forgotten to call him up, so I texted "In Barcelona safe, with family, told them about us." Quick response back "Great, a little late though…I calculated that you arrived about an hour ago XD Love you honey, talk tonight."

We were home now, quick shower while mom made us kids some pizza. The nights I spent at Gabriel´s hotel was regular couple nights, no sex come to think of it, but it was good like that. A relationship shouldn´t always be defined by whether you have sex or not, it should be about feelings towards each other.

It was a calm night at home with the family, later Gabriel was going to call but he had already been texting me since I left the airport. He was not at home resting though; he was working at the bar and tomorrow he was going to buy some furniture for the apartment.

The clock hit 11 pm and I woke up worried, I had missed his phone call at 9 and then at 9:30, 10 and 10:30. There was a text "I hope you´re asleep, if you don´t see this until tomorrow then I wish you a very good night. If you´re awake, call me, I just got back from the bar. Love G." I went to my bedroom and called him up, instant reply "Hey, I just got out of the shower. How are you darling?" I smiled to myself, it was good to hear his voice again, I remembered how much I missed talking to him although I was very tired. I sat on my bed and listened to how his day was, I could imagine him serving drinks, listening to music and I must've dozed off a little because he said "Hey, I'm going to let you get some sleep and we'll talk tomorrow? You can call me when you wake up, I'll probably be up before you anyway. Goodnight, babe, sleep tight." I was already very much asleep.

Monday morning, I was a little late for the closing of my office in central Barcelona and to wish my receptionist a very good luck in her new job. The guys from the DMV were thrilled to have her over and she fit right in, very efficient girl. On my way to the subway, I bumped into the one person I didn't need to see right now: Perry.

He was alone, wearing jeans and a sweater with a backpack. At first, he didn't notice that I was sitting right there on the bench, but he just had to sit next to me. He must've been looking at me because he moved closer and said "Why didn't you say hey to me? We're not strangers." I took off my earphones and looked him in the eyes, he had the same look on his face last time we saw each other "Hi Perry, are you well?" I said and he took my hands, squeezed them, noticing the ring on my right hand. "You´re still with him?" he said and let my hands go. "Yes, I´m with Gabriel and you´re with Natalie, right? We both got what we wanted."

He sighed heavily; this was apparently very difficult for him but our relationship didn´t work out. "We weren´t meant to be Perry, you need to accept that because I already did, and I moved on. You should too and if you aren´t with Natalie, find someone who can make you happy because that is what you need." I said and took the metro, he went in after me. The conductor must´ve hit the brakes because it stopped abruptly, and Perry grabbed my waist to prevent me from falling on the floor. "Uh, thanks." I said and found a seat, he sat in front of me, smiled like he used to when we were together.

"Where are you going?" he finally said after been smiling at me for a while, I felt the phone vibrate in my bag, that had to be Gabriel. "Work related." I said shortly, looked out the window. His eyes glittered and I couldn´t be mean to him, something in my heart couldn´t bear to see him sad "How's Natalie?" and he looked down to his shoes, looked up to me again and said "She is fine, had a baby, named Florence but she passed 4 days later, heart failure and now Natalie is going to therapy 3 times a week. She moved to the south of France to some aunt, and she helps her as well. It's been a rough couple of months but I make the most of it." What? How horrible, it wasn't that long ago that one of my former colleagues told me about them being together and I also saw them...poor kid.

"I'm sorry for your loss, I know that you cared for her." I said and he smiled weakly, that's when he looked endearing to me and said "I'm free in the worst possible way, the child wasn't mine, but I love her like she was, I suffered the same as if I was her father." I didn't know what to say, how can you comfort someone that's going through something like this? My phone rang again, and I sent a quick message "Babe, I'm with a friend that needs comforting. I'll call you after. XXX."

It wasn't a lie and I would tell him when I called him later, I took Perry's hand and said "I'm sorry for your loss, I can't imagine what you're going through but I know things happen for a reason and sometimes even though we don't understand." He put his other hand on mine and moved closer to me, I was feeling a little crowded, so I sat back. "I know, it´s just that I thought for a moment -now I´m free to look you up and now that you´re here, I feel you more distant than ever." My lips were a line, my chapter with Perry was closed and sorry to say not even this terrible moment could move me away from Gabriel. I tried again "I´m sorry Perry, we had our moment and I don´t regret it but I love him. I know that you one day might find the one for you and then you can finally begin a new life. Give yourself a chance."

I gave him a quick hug, got up from the seat and made myself ready to exit at the next station "Universitat". For the third time in my life, I left him and now it was for good, he didn´t have to know that I was moving across the Baltic Sea. I called up Gabriel, he was worried "Hey, sorry, I bumped into someone I wasn´t ready to see. Yes, my ex.

No nothing out of the ordinary, of course I did, we took the metro, but he continued and I´m now at Universitat. Yes, okay after the meeting though. Love you too, bye." I walked towards the DMV to leave the last things belonging to my receptionist plus a little gift, she was feeling at home there and thanked me for the period we worked together.

Left the DMV and called Gabriel again, he had the night off because he had helped the owner to move some things to the basement. But the cheekiness in his voice surely made their point "Are you free tonight? I was thinking we could chat tonight; you know live and see each other. What do you say?" I smiled to myself, sure that could be nice, so I said yes. That's when he reminded me "You will have to lock your door though, it might get too hot unless..." My cheeks were burning, what was he planning to do now?

"Unless you want to go to a hotel tonight and celebrate us?" a voice behind me said and I turned around: there he was, live like he said. I hugged him tight, he kissed me and then I said, "But how?" He chuckled "I came back this morning, since you told me that you were going to the DMV I hung around until I saw you walking out. Come on, let's have a coffee."

We walked together to the closest coffee shop and ordered, walked out and I said, "So what are your plans for us tonight?" he took my hand and we walked through the streets of a cold

Barcelona. He smirked at me but didn´t say anything, we suddenly stopped at the department store "El Corte Ingles". Up the stairs to the women's department, he went straight up to the cashier and said, "Excuse me, I called and put away a dress last week under the name Gabriel." The girl checked in the closet behind her where they put all the layaways and took out a lavender dress in a big bag. He received it and gave it to me "This is yours and I need you to change." I stared at him, the dress was beautifully cut, just below the knee and very simple, just the way I liked it. Before I went to the changing room he said "Don´t forget the shoes, they should work with your taste and the dress."

He said and handed me a box of Vans, inside a pair of lavender flats in their most popular kind. I smiled all the way to the changing room, changed and couldn´t stop crying in silence when I saw myself in the mirror. I looked unusually beautiful, even without make-up. Outside he said, "Are you ready?" I held my breath and said "Yeah, you can open the curtain." There he was in a white shirt, first 2 buttons opened, black suit pants and black shiny shoes. He looked like James Bond´s better looking brother in his black hair, brown eyes, and slightly curly hair. His eyes watered when he saw me, his hand stretched out to reach mine and he finally said, "You look marvelous, come on we have one more stop to do." We passed by the cashier, and she smiled to us both, my bag with clothes was heavy and he took it until we reached the street, and he popped the trunk of a car parked in the street. "Is this yours?" I said and he opened the door to the passenger seat, while he went to the drivers end "No, it´s a rental. When we get back to Edinburgh I´ll get one for us, don´t you worry my dear." Gabriel drove away and stopped outside the catholic church in central Barrio Gotic, parked around the corner and we got out.

I still didn´t understand until I saw them in the entrance of the church, my family, in nice outfits. "Uh honey, what are we...?" I began and he took both my hands in his, saying "I don´t want to spend another day without you being my proper wife, that´s why we´re getting married today, with your family as our witnesses."

W E D D I N G   B E L L S

I was shocked but happy, it was such a beautiful surprise. With tears in my eyes, my hair messy and no make-up we got married in the church. Among the little crowd of family was my grandma, who gave me a hug and handed me a watch in silver "Here honey, wear this, it´s your something old." I smiled, she helped me put it on and I continued walking towards the altar with Gabriel by my side.

We hugged people along the way until we saw the priest waiting for us. Suddenly I heard a familiar song in the background: Goo Goo Dolls "Iris" and the tears were running. "We´re gathered here today to join two people in holy matrimony. They came together, by their free will and will be joined together freely by the grace of God. Today, his daughter Graciela Elena will join Gabriel Andrés in holy union. What God unites; man cannot separate. The rings please." On my side, my sister had his and on his side the bartender from Edinburgh had mine. He took it, gave him a nod and placed the ring on my left finger with the words "I, Gabriel Andrés Demiurgos take thee Graciela Elena García to be my wife. To love, honor and humor all my life." I took a deep breath to keep from crying and received the ring from my sister "I, Graciela Elena García take thee Gabriel Andrés Demiurgos to be my husband, in good and bad times, to love, honor and humor all my life."

The priest smiled and said "Well with these beautiful vows, although unusual I pronounce you husband and wife. I give you the new Mr. and Mrs. Demiurgos." We kissed and the crowd cheered, he whispered "I love you, so much and wouldn´t have done it any other way." I was happy to be married like this: just family and that he also planned it with them. He shouted, "Wedding dinner is at Guanabara, let´s go!" The restaurant was a Brazilian BBQ with a special twist, there was something for everyone: meats, pasta, vegetarian and fish.

As we approached the parking lot, the guests already inside, he stayed out with me a short while. I tried to read the look on his face, something in between worry and happiness, I reached for his cheek and said, "What is it?". He put his arms around me, breathed in my scent (the little perfume I had left since most of it went in my regular clothes) and he reached in his pocket, a little box. "For you, now that we´re married, you can have these." I took it and opened; it was a set of keys. "Where do these go? I said and we began walking slowly to the restaurant, he smiled underneath his breath and said proudly "They go to *our apartment* in Edinburgh, while you were here in Barcelona, I called in a favor and my friend managed to leave the place fit for a woman like you. Now we can live together, as husband and wife."

His eyes welled up, he pulled me close and sniffed on my shoulder, I couldn´t hold it anymore and my tears also began to run down my cheeks. "Listen to me, dear husband of mine: I wouldn´t care if we lived in a trailer as long as we do it together. Thank you so much for this beautiful gift and I look forward living there with *you*. Now, can we go and celebrate with our family?" We kissed and walked inside to the already celebrating party. Dinner and dessert for everyone until late night, people laughing and enjoying themselves.

I took a good look at Gabriel: the once little boy without family, with so much love and will power to make things work, that rose from the ashes to a self-employed man that had now become my husband and the love of my life. My eyes watered as I did my first toast as a married woman and my husband dried his tears in absolute silence. He rose from the seat, pulled me into his arms and said, "I love you, my heart and soul, I love you." Everyone cheered and we decided to leave for our long journey back to Edinburgh with certain stops along the way. Our honeymoon would wait, he needed to work, and I needed to set up my decoration firm there.

My dress was perfect for the motorcycle ride, Gabriel had gotten me a black leather jacket as a wedding gift, and I think I´ve never felt sexier than right there. Our stops went through Andorra, Bordeaux (where we stayed in this beautiful vineyard), walked through the beach at the feet of Mount St Michel (where we took some pretty pictures) until we concluded in Calais to travel to the UK. Luckily the weather worked with us, and the sun shined through London and all the way to our home in Edinburgh.

I had never seen our home, since when I left, he was still working on it, but it was beautiful: it was above the bar where he worked, with a nice view in the back to a park. A big kitchen and living room, our bedroom had a big window with a sill to sit on with view over the square outside. "It´s beautiful, I love it, I love you!" I said and hugged him; he was very pleased with himself. "We can buy something bigger when we have more money, a house with a yard, what do you think?" I nodded, caressed his head with his dark curly hair, he was getting tiny strains of white, my hands moved to his slightly beardy cheeks. I pulled him close so I could kiss him, gently at first, careful, but he understood me, so he just drew me closer. Gabriel smelt like the first morning breeze, his lips tasted eucalyptus, his tongue carefully found its way in and found mine. He sighed deeply, took one of my breaths with me and walked with me in his arms to the closest wall, which was good since I was losing my footing and he needed to have me still. His lips moved to my neck, and I felt my entire spine rise in chills, I wrapped my arms around his neck as he pulled up my sweatshirt, chuckled a little when my head got stuck and got very happy that I was only wearing a bra underneath. "I believe sir, it´s my turn. You´re too dressed up." I said quietly and he stood still, when I unbuttoned the black shirt, he was wearing, the one I bought in Bordeaux, because black just suits him. I moved my face to his collar, to expose his bare neck that smelled of Burberry Brit apart from his natural fresh scent. My heated lips formed around it, kissing gently and his hand holding on to me while caressing my bare back. I pulled away, just enough to see him, before I went back to his lips.

He moved away with me to the bed, gently putting me down, while I took off his shirt. The smiles between us were like wires, connecting every cell in our bodies to that moment, our moment, until he unbuttoned my jeans and I his black pants. "There isn´t enough time to love you, but I´ll settle with as long as I live. I love you, Grace."

I heard music coming from the kitchen, not too loud but it gave me a sense of comfort since I realized that I was there, in our home and in our bed. I reached to check the alarm clock on my side, not that I put the alarm to wake up but just to see how much I had slept.

There was a silky robe right next to the bed, on a chair and a little piece of paper on top: "When you wake up, wear this and come to the kitchen XOXO". I smiled, put it on and followed the smell of freshly baked bread to the kitchen. There was Gabriel, buttering bread and putting it on a plate with different cold cuts, serving tea. He was only wearing his boxers, I enjoyed looking at his back because there was something particularly handsome about him standing there. "I thought I heard your footsteps." He said and turned around, I gave him a guilty smile and he came over with the plates "Good morning wife, how was your night?". We kissed and I slid up my hand to touch his bare chest, there weren´t many men who could pull off being this clean shaved. Well, he didn´t have to shave, he just didn´t have hair on his chest and for me, much better. I beamed at him "Very well, although slightly sore, the ride on the bike was a bit intense." He smirked and said "Easy", I chuckled, he must have thought of last night, but it was perfect. I drifted away, to that moment and he brought me back by moving a little of my robe to expose my shoulder. I wasn´t cold but his touch surely made my skin turn into chicken skin, he knew what he was doing. "We should eh, have breakfast first. Then you should shower and get dressed because I must do some soundcheck for tonight, the owner Dave gave me a singing spot."

I sighed, he licked his lips and reached out to kiss me.

Gabriel was doing the dishes while I had my shower and now, I was putting the remaining bread in bags to freeze. I admired him, all wrapped up in his thoughts when I went over to wrap my arms around him. He was still in his boxers, a little cold and I needed to warm him up by taking off my shirt, placing my nose towards his spine. "Hey honey, everything okay?" he said and turned around, a little confused since he had seen me fully clothed earlier. I pulled him close to a fervently kiss, he tried to say something but I didn't let him, suddenly he got a chance to talk "My beautiful wife, I have to finish here and then get ready for the soundcheck. Trust me, I would love to stay with you, but we need to go." I pouted but gave him another quick kiss, as I reached for my blouse on the floor, he was looking at my boobs almost falling out of the bra and said loudly "My God woman!"

He grabbed my waist, pulled me up in his arms and carried me to the bedroom. I laughed quietly in his ear; my little coup worked!

"What are you singing tonight?" I said and pressed my nose against his, he still smelt fresh, and that minty taste was still on my body. He pressed an innocent kiss on my forehead and said "I don´t know yet, he did tell me that he would lend me a guitar, but you know, I haven´t played in years. What do you think? What would you like me to play?" I thought for a moment, anything would sound perfect because he truly had a beautiful voice: he was singing in the morning when we were in Bordeaux, a song by Edith Piaf "La Foule" and wow. "I would love to hear David Bowie´s Heroes, it´s one of my favorites. And if you can´t, use the guitar well you could just sing, no need for props."

Gabriel´s mouth searched for mine for a kiss, I heard him moan "Mmm" and I laughed a little. We stayed in bed for a while, got up and he got ready for his show downstairs. I followed, put on a pair of jeans and the blouse that started it all. He came to my side to help me with the silver chain with a little feather I got from my sister for the wedding, he removed my hair to the side and kissed my neck carefully, trying to hook it but left it on the table instead.

Gabriel spun me around, his lips locked on mine and suddenly he was unbuttoning my blouse "Mm babe, didn't you say you needed to be downstairs in 30 minutes?" I said but he just kept going "Yeah but we got time." "I surrender then." I said and he sat down with me on top, his pants were unbuttoned but I removed them in no time to leave him in his boxers. My panties were still on, and he pulled me up a little to take them off, then he sat me back in his erected penis peeking out of the boxers.

"Oh baby..." he said to my ear as he moved, kissed, and breathed loudly. I tried to keep up, it was getting too hot and soon I wasn't able to keep it together any longer. While he was kissing me, he noticed that my bra was still on and unhooked it, throwing it on the floor. My breasts were aroused, his touch only enhanced the feeling and I pressed myself towards his naked torso. His hands held on to my back, moved down to my butt and then back up again, my head rested on his shoulder, breathless.

"Well, I think we uh, should get a quick shower and head downstairs?" he said and gave me a passionate kiss, I smiled towards him and got up. "Oh, and since we´re in a hurry, we should probably save some water, right?" he winked, of course we do.

SEVENTEEN

GABRIEL & THE ANGELIC VOICE

"From Barcelona, with love, I give you Gabriel!" shouted the bartender and the crowd cheered, I was standing by the right side of the stage close to one of the bouncers. There sure was a lot of women tonight and since my husband looked mighty fine, I wouldn't be surprised if one approached him with intention to chat.

He looked sure of himself onstage, maybe this was his dream, to sing for a crowd. His guitar, a Gibson 2000 was connected to the amplifiers and suddenly his voice shut the whole place down: he was singing "If I ever leave this world". It had been a while since I last saw a crowd go wild, I think it was at the Justin Timberlake 20/20 tour that the women went nuts. I was happy for him, he really liked this, suddenly he gave me a look and I just smiled back. "This woman right here, is the reason I sing, she's my wife and I love her, this baby, is for you: this is Heroes!"

"I, I will be king

And you, you will be queen (he pointed at me)

Though nothing will drive them away

We can beat them, just for one day

We can be Heroes, just for one day…"

He sang my favorite Bowie song and I couldn´t hold back the tears, all cred to Bowie for creating this song but Gabriel´s voice…angelic.

It was a hot night; the bar was packed and people ordering drinks from here to there. It was now 2 am and my knees were really in need to rest, I´m beginning to think that the night life isn´t made for me because at midnight usually is when I go to bed. I rested my head against the doorframe and a pair of hands suddenly wrapped in my waist "Hello you, time to go home?" His voice surpassed the blurring sound of people talking, laughing, and shouting, I turned against his chest and buried my face in it murmuring "Yeah, I´m very much tired." He held my back, stroked it, and whispered in my ear "Let´s get out of here then, come on." We said goodnight to the bartender, the bouncers high fived Gabriel and walked up the stairs to our apartment.

I went straight to the bathroom, brushed my teeth, and changed clothes. As I was about to take my pajamas, I saw a silky negligee hanging in the closet and thought that maybe this could be convenient tonight although I was way too tired for any misbehavior. Went for the comfy pajamas, Gabriel was in the kitchen making some hot tea for us, had already stripped to his pajama pants but no shirt yet. I took a deep breath, admired him from a distance, thinking how much he meant to me as a person: he's my husband, my best friend, my lover, my companion, and I love him, so much. A tear escaped my eye and I wiped it, to make sure he didn't see it but he had already been glancing at me, he came over and put his arms around me. "Hey, hey...what's the matter?" I smiled at him, nodded that it was nothing and we went to the sofa where he curled up with me in his arms. "Ahh my love, don't be sad, tell me, what's going on?" I wiped my tears and said, "I don't actually know, it was just a feeling in my chest that I've never really felt before." He caressed my arms, kissed my head and said "Well, I need you to know something...I love you. No other woman could ever make me feel the way you do, if you feel threatened by the screaming women downstairs, they don't matter."

I fell asleep in his arms, to the soothing sound of his voice humming a quiet tune.

"So, Gabriel, how´s the married life? Wife´s keep you on a short leash?" said the bartender while drying some glasses, Gabriel wasn´t paying attention since he was going through the finances from the night before. They did pretty good each night when he sang, they were really packing them in. £1500 for each night that he had a show and since they had special entrance fee when he performed, he got 50% of the profits including consumption. Apart from his salary of course, so he did very good.

I had opened my décor firm in a nearby office, since it was a 9 am to 4 pm job I had plenty of time to be with him when he sound checked and on Fridays, I stayed to watch his show. It was a popular day, mostly because people loved coming here to get their drink on but also because most women found Gabriel attractive.

Still at the office, going through some papers for a development of a new department store and it had been taking up a lot of time, so much that I had been skipping lunch a few times a week to have more time to work on it.

It was now 4:45 pm and I still couldn't get away, today was Friday and I knew Gabriel was having his sound check at 5 pm but there was no way I could get there in time. He understood though, since he had supported me during my restart and now, I could finally help more in our monthly payments. He called at 4:59 pm "Hey honey, you alright? Where are you? The soundcheck is in 5 more minutes, do you think you'll make it?" I sighed; this was the third time that I wasn't available to see him. "I'm sorry honey, I can't. Still at work and this thing is driving me nuts, I'll be home soon and I'll be at the show later, okay?" I waited for his response, but I only heard him breath loudly and suddenly he shouted "Well, since you don't find what I do important, maybe you could skip everything instead." And hung up.

Why was he being a baby about this? The show is always more important than the soundcheck, he never spoke to me like this but honestly, I didn't have time to deal with this now. I continued my work and finally had a breakthrough finishing at exactly 6:30 pm, so happy until I checked my desk calendar and see "Hubby's birthday party at 5 pm. Get cake!". Oh...crap.... I forgot his birthday, he turned 42 today! No, how could I be so stupid?? He's never going to forgive me, what could I do?

I grabbed my bag and locked the door, ran out to see if the nearby bakery was opened and it was!! Went in and asked "Hi, do you have any chocolate cakes available? I need 3 with the text Happy Birthday Gabriel, 42." The girl behind the counter said that she only had 2 chocolate and one fromage, so she offered me a discount for them which I accepted also because she wanted to close with most things sold. The decoration of his name and age she threw in for free, so I paid and thanked her. Called a cab out in the street to get there and to my surprise the bar was closed to the public.

There was a sign on the door "Closed for private party, come back tomorrow from 7 pm until 4 am." I walked to the side door, where I took out my keys to open, this was the original entrance for us but since Gabriel was tight with the owner we could go through the bar. I managed to get in with the cakes intact, passed through the hallway and peeked in through the window at the party inside. Suddenly I saw Gabriel, standing on the bar counter with a microphone in his hand, I felt guilty by forgetting his birthday, but I had gotten him a nice present a while ago and now it was my chance to use it.

A woman I had never seen before climbed on top of the counter and planted a kiss on Gabriel's lips, he looked surprised but didn't exactly push her away. My heart bursts into flames of anger and disappointment and I just couldn't take the sight of him with someone else. I ran up the stairs, chucked the cakes in the fridge and went to take a shower. There I let my anger go, I cried for a while and then I could finally breathe. I put on my home clothes, warmed up some leftovers from the night before and wrapped myself in a blanket in front of the tv.

The phone turned its lights on, a text message had arrived from Gabriel "Hey, are you home? There's cake and food in the bar for you, I'll be waiting. I'm sorry for being an idiot before, I miss you. Call me or text, love you." I didn't respond anything, but I did go to the wardrobe and found one of my more festive dresses: a black halter neck dress with a pair of black ballerinas. My hair was finally complying to the hair mousse, and I looked like a million bucks, which was my weapon of choice for his party. There was Gabriel standing by the bar, his back turned against the door where I came in from, talking to the owner. He saw me and waved me over, Gabriel turned around and he came towards me with quick steps.

Before I said anything, he hugged me tightly and said "Baby, I´m sorry. I´m so sorry, are you okay?" I patted his back, by the look on his face he did look sad and remorseful for what he yelled over the phone. But the image of that woman kissing him and he not putting much of a resistance bothered me more than I wanted to admit. "I´m okay, can we go someplace quiet and talk?" I said and he gave me a worried nod showing me towards the owner's office. Gabriel let me in first, opened a bottle of soda and served me a drink. He took a smaller glass of Scotch and sat down with me in the sofa, took a deep breath and said "Honey, I´m sorry, I was worried sick. Where did you go after work?" I took a sip, looked serious and said, "I went to get cakes from the bakery but I didn´t know that you had planned a party and I definitely didn´t know you had such a gift prepared."

He winced, like I had struck a nerve and he knew exactly what I was talking about "I´m as surprised as you, it was my day off, I was supposed to pick you up but then Fredricks asked me to help him and then it was a bunch of people there. And about the woman who kissed me, it was the bouncer's girlfriend Jennie.

She had one too many, became a little overfriendly and they couldn't stop her. I told you, you're the only one for me." Gabriel was telling the truth and I felt dumb, he had a lot of time to be with others if he wanted to but instead, he stayed faithful to me. He put his arm around me, and I moved closer, suddenly he let go, got up, saying "Hey, by the way, that dress...where did you get it?" I gave him a goofy smile, got up and gave him 360 degrees look of me. He took my hand, whirled me around and I ended up in his arms "So, what cake did you get?" His nose pressed against mine and I took a deep sigh, he got all excited and whispered "Easy..." giving me a little smile.

We said goodnight to Fredricks, ran up the stairs and went directly to the fridge and checked the cakes: "Chocolate or raspberry?" I said and he grabbed my waist, turned me around, realizing he was naked "How about both? Oh and, don't bring spoons." I laughed a little, cut 2 pieces, one of each cake and went after him to the bedroom. I put the plate down and asked "So, what are we doing with the cake?" He stood in front of me, trying to undress me by unhooking the clasp of my halter neck, kissed my exposed neck and let the top fall to my waist. "You smell so good.

You have no idea how sorry I am for what I said earlier, it was a stupid behavior and I´m a stupid man. Forgive me, I don´t deserve this beautiful gift that is you and neither do I deserve the cakes." I pulled him close to me, I could feel his warm body against mine still slightly dressed, his erection pressing with only my dress in the way. Moving my hands towards his face, I looked him in the eyes and said "I´m sorry too, work has been taking up most of my time and I didn´t even check the calendar just in case, but now I finally caught a break and after that payment we could go somewhere. What do you think?" He sneaked in a smile and finished off my dress, so there I was standing in my black panties and strapless bra. A cheeky smile, in his mind I was already naked but still he wanted to admire me from a short distance, I kicked my dress that was in a pile at my feet to the side. Gabriel grabbed my naked waist, I had to hold on to him, not to fall but I didn´t want him to continue removing my underwear just yet.

Like we did back then, when we spent a lot of time teasing each other, I wanted to give him a taste of his own medicine: I walked away and took off my strapless bra slowly, he just watched in awe and widened his visage of me when my panties disappeared.

I sat on the bed, like a muse waiting to be painted when he came to my side to seduce me into a session of love and cake.

Happy birthday husband, I love you.

EIGHTEEN

THE FINAL SURPRISE

"Tea, my dear?" he said and poured up a cup as I cut some of the cake for us. It had been 2 days since his birthday and the cakes where on their last run, I smiled, now fully dressed in my pajama shirt and shorts. Gabriel was wearing his pajama pants but no shirt, on my request: I liked looking at him, his complexion was just perfect in tone with his slightly pale skin that he looked like those marble statues that you see at the British Museum or even the Louvre.

"Ugh, today´s Sunday…which means tomorrow´s Monday and then it´s back to work again. I hope the payment comes in soon, I can´t wait to get away with you." I said and rested my head against his bare chest, tapping quietly on his stomach. He smiled, drinking his tea, and then placing a kiss on top of my head. "Where do you want to go? If we could go anywhere?" he said and held me tightly while I thought for a moment.

Suddenly, in between thinking about a location where we could go on vacation, I felt this weird feeling in my stomach. Maybe the cakes weren't so good anymore, because holding my mouth to avoid vomiting all over the bed, I ran to the bathroom. He came right after me, bringing a wet towel to wipe my sweaty face. "Are you okay? Come here, ohh baby." I took a deep breath, tried not to move too close to him, just in case it was food poisoning. "No, don't move close to me. I don't want you to get sick, would you mind throwing away the cakes? Oh, is there any Omeprazole or maybe Pepto in the cupboard? Could you bring me some?" He looked so concerned, went to get the medication and a glass of water. We sat for a while on the bathroom floor and his concern only grew when a week later, my stomach had not recovered. Gabriel called a clinic, and we took a cab there, because I couldn't walk properly without feeling lousy.

The doctor, a slightly older man, took my blood pressure, ordered some exams, and told us to wait outside in the waiting area for a while. I looked out the window thinking what could've happened to me during this time, but nothing came to mind apart from the excessive cake eating when the doctor called my name.

I went in and Gabriel was right behind me, but he told him that he could wait outside, he went back to his seat, and I gave him a quick kiss on the cheek. Doctor T. Butler let me in first, closed the door behind me and said, "Sit down miss, let´s see your results." His Scottish accent was bulletproof, I could barely understand him but when he suddenly smiled and said, "Congratulations lassie, you´ll be adding another little person to your family." I didn´t understand, I was in my early 40´s and couldn´t possibly be...*pregnant*?? I had to ask "How can it be? I´m too old to have kids, besides isn´t it dangerous to have children after 35?" He took off his glasses and said "We´ll be monitoring you, you´ll come to check-up once a week, every 2 weeks during the whole pregnancy. Here´s a recipe for folic acid that you can get from the local pharmacy, see you in 2 weeks and congratulations again lassie. You´ll be a great *mother*..."

I took the paper, took my jacket, and walked out. Gabriel was drinking coffee from the vending machine by the nurses' station, the one we passed on the way in when he saw me. He came towards me and helped me put on my jacket, took my hand and we walked out of the building. We were quiet for some time, and he suddenly broke the silence "It´s bad, isn´t it? Are you dying?"

I saw tears in the corner of his eyes, and we stopped by a bench in the nearby park, he was already sniffing, thinking the worse and I didn´t know how to break it down to him.

"No honey, I´m not dying. But this surely changes things, perspective and that trip we were supposed to take when my payment comes. Maybe we won´t be able to make it." I said and he looked even more confused than before, he held my hand in a tight grip "Tell me, if you´re not dying, are you sick in some other way or do you want to leave me?" I smiled weakly; we had never talked about having more family than us two. Since he had a difficult childhood, maybe he thought of having children would mean less love for him, I have no idea.

Suddenly I smiled, he was calming down and I looked deeply into his eyes "Gabriel, I´m pregnant. You´re going to be a father, to our child." The look on his face changed in slow motion: from serious, to surprised, to a tiny smile, to the biggest smile, to tears of joy and then he spoke "I´m going to be a daddy? The daddy to your kid? Our kid??" I smiled back, nodded and now everything was back to normal speed: He grabbed my waist, pulled me up in his arms, kissed me all over the face and then put me down, went down on his knees to pull up my shirt to expose my belly.

It didn´t look like much but to think that there was a baby in there, *our baby*.

EPILOGUE

"Please welcome to 2047´s New York bookfair, our guest of honor, the always enchanting Luna Demiurgos!!" the filled saloon cheered, like a wave from corner to corner. Her photo was in their biggest posters, her name was on the screen behind the presenter in her favorite font: Cezanne.

At the same time, in a small room, with a little window, there was a young, dark-haired woman gathering her thoughts. She took one last look in the mirror by the door and suddenly heard a quiet knock. A woman entered and said: "Miss? It´s time." She nodded at her and said to her reflection "Showtime" before walking out. A man behind the stage greeted her, handing over a silverplated microphone and she mouthed a thank you. She walked up the stairs, smiled big and said to herself "Mom, dad, this is for you."

In the background you could hear: From Yesterday by 30 STM

BONUS: PLAYLIST

KELIS "TRICK ME" (COMPANY X-MAS PARTY)

EUROPE "OPEN YOUR HEART" (GRACE & PERRY)

HIM "PRETENDING" (NATALIE & PERRY)

LUIS FONSI FEAT. DADDY YANKEE "DESPACITO" (SEDUCTION)

FANTASTIC BEASTS & THE CRIMES OF THE GRINDELWALD "LETA´S THEME (CAR RIDE)

BOYZONE "WORDS" (CAR RIDE 2)

SHAKIRA "TE DEJO MADRID" (GOING TO SEVILLA)

LENNY KRAVITZ "ARE YOU GONNA GO MY WAY" (MEETING GABRIEL)

ANNIE LENNOX "WHY" (LEAVING)

HOZIER "TAKE ME TO CHURCH" (WEDDING BELLS)

GARY BARLOW "SO HELP ME GIRL" (MARRIAGE IN BARCELONA)

ADELE "SKYFALL" (MOTORCYCLE RIDE)

SAM SMITH "THE WRITING'S ON THE WALL" (EDINBURGH)

GEORGE MICHAEL "DON'T LET THE SUN GO DOWN ON ME" (BAR SONGS)

DAVID BOWIE "HEROES" (BAR SONGS 2 DEDICATED)

TEN SHARP "YOU" (MISSED BIRTHDAY)

30 STM "FROM YESTERDAY" (LUNA)

DAVID BOWIE "REBEL REBEL" (ENDING)